D1860146

HADJI MURÁD

HADJI MURÁD

BY

LEO TOLSTOY

Author of "Anna Karenina,"
"Resurrection," etc.

TRANSLATED BY AYLMER MAUDE

Frontispiece

©Author

All rights reserved. No part of this work may be reproduced, stored, adapted, or transmitted in any form or by any means, electronic, mechanical, photocopying, micro-filming recording or otherwise, or translated in any language, without the prior written permission of the copyright owner and the publisher. The book is sold subject to the condition that it shall not, by way of trade or otherwise, be lent, resold, hired out, or otherwise circulated without the prior publisher's written consent in any form of binding or cover other than that in which it is published.

The views and opinions expressed in this book are author(s) own and the facts reported by them have been verified to the extent possible, and the publishers are not in any way liable for the same.

ISBN: 978-93-5128-537-3

First Published in 1912
Indian Reprint in 2017

Published by

Kalpaz Publications
C-30, Satyawati Nagar,
Delhi – 110052
E-mail: kalpaz@hotmail.com
Website: kalpazpublications.com
Ph.: +91-9212142040

Cataloging in Publication Data—DK
Courtesy: D.K. Agencies (P) Ltd. <docinfo@dkagencies.com>

Tolstoy, Leo, *graf,* 1828-1910, **author.**
[Khadzhi-Murat. English]
Hadji Murád/by Leo Tolstoy; translated by Aylmer Maude.
pages cm
Novel.
Translated from Russian.
"First published in 1912"—Title page verso.
ISBN 9789351285373

1. Historical fiction, Russian—Translations into English. I. Maude, Aylmer, 1858-1938, translator. II. Title.

PG3366.K5 2017 DDC 891.733 23

PREFACE

"I am writing to you specially to say how glad I have been to be your contemporary, and to express my last and sincere request. My friend, return to literary activity! That gift came to you from whence comes all the rest.... Great writer of our Russian land, listen to my wish!"

So wrote Turgenev on his deathbed to Tolstoy, when the latter, absorbed in religious struggles and studies, had for five years produced no work of art save one short story.

Nor was it long before the wish was realised, for three years later Tolstoy was writing "The Death of Ivan Ilyitch," and that tremendous drama, "The Power of Darkness"; and these were followed by a number of short stories, some plays, a long novel (" Resurrection ") and the works now posthumously published. Among these latter a foremost place belongs to "Hadji Murad," in which Tolstoy again tells of that Caucasian life which supplied him with the matter for some of his earliest tales as well as for his great story "The Cossacks," which Turgenev declared to be ''the best story that has been written in our (Russian) language."

The Caucasus indeed offered a rich variety of material on which Tolstoy drew at every stage of his literary career. It was there that, at the age of twenty-three, he first saw war as a volunteer; there he served for two years as a cadet ; and there finally he became an officer, before leaving to serve in the Crimean war—which in its turn gave him material for his sketches of "Sevastopol."

In his letters from the Caucasus he often complained of the dulness and emptiness of his life there; yet it certainly attracted him for a while, and was not devoid of stirring and curious incidents.

The most extraordinary of these relates to a gambling debt he incurred and was unable to pay. Having given notes-of-hand, he was in despair when the date of payment approached without his having been able to procure the money needed, and he prayed earnestly to God "to get me out of this disagreeable scrape."

The very next morning he received a letter enclosing his notes-of-hand, which were returned to him as a free gift by a young Chechen named Sado, who had become his kunak (devoted friend) and had won them back at cards from the officer who won them from Tolstoy.

It was in company with that same Sado that Tolstoy, when passing from one fort to another, was chased by the enemy and nearly captured.

His life was in imminent danger on another occasion, when a shell, fired by the enemy, smashed the carriage of a cannon he was pointing; but once again he escaped unhurt.

It was during his first year in the Caucasus that Tolstoy began writing for publication. "The Raid," describing the kind of warfare he was witnessing there, was the second of his stories to appear in print. A little later he wrote two other tales dealing with the same subject: "The Wood-Felling," and ''Meeting a Moscow Acquaintance in the Detachment."

Feeling that he had not exhausted the material at his disposal, he then planned "The Cossacks: a Caucasian Story of 1852," which he kept on hand unfinished for nearly ten years, and might not have published even then had he not happened to lose some money at Chinese billiards to a stranger he met at the club in Moscow. To pay this debt, he sold ''The Cossacks" for Rs. 1,000 (about £150 in those days) to Katkov, the well-known publicist and publisher, with whom he subsequently quarrelled. The circumstances under which he had parted with "The Cossacks" were so unpleasant to Tolstoy that he never completed the story.

Ten years later, when he had set his heart on producing an attractive reading-book for children, he wrote the charming little story "A Prisoner in the Caucasus" (one of the gems in "Twenty-three Tales"), founded on the abovementioned incident of his own narrow escape from capture; and finally, after another thirty years had passed, he drew upon his Caucasian recollections for the last time when he composed "Hadji Murad."

Tolstoy had met Hadji Murad in Tiflis in December 1851,[1] and in a letter addressed to his brother Sergius on the 23rd of that month he wrote,—

"If you wish to show off with news from the Caucasus, you may recount that a certain Hadji Murad (second in importance to Shamil himself) surrendered a few days ago to the Russian Government. He was the leading daredevil and 'brave' of all Chechnya, but has been led into committing a mean action."

The details of Hadji Murad 's life as given by Tolstoy in his story are not always historically exact ; but the main events are true, and the tale is told in a way that gives a vivid and faithful picture of those stirring times.

Of the struggle for independence carried on in the Caucasus with such desperate bravery for so many years, very little was known to English readers until the publication of Mr. Baddeley's "The Russian Conquest of the Caucasus," which gives an excellent account of that involved, confusing and long drawn-out, but important, contest.

---

1. Writing my "Life of Tolstoy" before I knew the full story of Hadji Murad, I confused him, in the first edition, with some one else, and stated that Tolstoy met him at Karalyk in 1871. On reading my book the Countess Tolstoy warned me of this mistake, but her warning did not reach me soon enough, and I was only able to put the matter right in a later edition.

The Caucasus is peopled by so many tribes, differing so much among themselves, and all so strange to Western Europeans, that it is not easy to summarise the history of the conflict in a way at once correct and clear. There are, however, certain main facts which should be borne in mind when reading "Hadji Murad."

As her only possible way of escape from the oppression of Persia on one side and of Turkey on another, Christian Georgia—lying to the south of the Caucasian Mountains—submitted to Eussia as long ago as the commencement of the nineteenth century.

Even before that Russia had spasmodically attempted to conquer the northern part of the Caucasus; but from then onwards she had a special incentive to press forward and annex the territories dividing her from Georgia which was already hers.

The internecine feuds of the native tribes generally prevented them from offering a united resistance to Russian aggression; but the dense forests of Chechnya, and the exceedingly mountainous character of Daghestan, rendered the subjugation of those regions a matter of great difficulty.

In addition to the geographical obstacles there was another, due to a strong religious revival which sprang up among the Mohammedan population and, despite the feuds among the tribes, to a considerable extent and for a considerable time united them in a holy war against the infidel Russians.

Like all great religious movements this revival had roots in a distant past. It also had currents, religious and political, which swept now in one direction and now in another.

To begin with, there was a Murid movement which appears to have been almost identical with Sufi'ism, and to have existed from the third century of the Mohammedan era. That movement, going beyond the Shariat (the written law), inculcated the Tarikat (the Path) leading to the higher life. It also proclaimed the equality of all Mussulmans, rich and poor alike, and enjoined temperance, abstinence, self-denial, and the renunciation of the good things of both worlds, that man may make himself "free to receive worthily the love towards God." In Muridism a teacher was called a Murshid ("one who shows" the way), while a Murid was a disciple or follower ("one who desires" to find the way).

Such was Muridism for several centuries: a peaceful, religious movement of a highly spiritual character ; but within the last few generations the struggle against Russia had given a new quality to the movement, and from being spiritual it had become strongly political.

As early as 1785 Mansur, a leader of unknown origin, appeared in the Caucasus preaching the Ghazavat, or Holy War, against the infidels; and from 1830 onwards, when Kazi-Mulla, the first Imam (uniting in himself supreme spiritual and temporal power) took the field, Muridism became identified with the fierce struggle for independence carried on by the native tribes against the Russian invaders.

Mansur and Kazi-Mulla are both mentioned in Tolstoy's story, in which also Hadji Murad tells of the part he took in the execution or assassination of Kazi-Mulla 's successor, Hamzad. Shamil, too, who succeeded Hamzad and was the greatest of the Imams, figures as one of the principal characters in the story.

How little the nature and importance of that war in the Caucasus was understood by Western Europe is shown by the fact that when the Crimean War broke out—the year after Hadji Murad's death—no serious attempt was made to support or encourage Shamil in the struggle which, even after the conclusion of the Crimean War, he desperately maintained against Russia till his last fortress fell in 1859, and he himself was sent prisoner to Kaluga.

We may be said to owe the existence of this story to the severe illnesses from which Tolstoy suffered in 1901 and 1902, for his sickness kept him in a state in which he found it difficult to work at "What is Religion?" or the other didactic essays he was engaged upon, and by way of relaxation he turned to fiction and produced ''Hadji Murad." It is worth noticing that in the fifth chapter of this—one of the last stories he ever wrote —Tolstoy describes a skirmish and a soldier's death in a way that closely reminds one of an incident he had handled in "The Wood Felling," nearly half a century before. He thus, at the outset and at the close of his literary career, told almost the same tale in almost the same way and with almost the same feeling.

On comparing the Caucasian stories he wrote between the ages of twenty-three and thirty-four with the one he wrote when he was seventy-four, one finds in them all the same wonderfully acute power of observation which seized the characteristic indications both of the inner and the outer life of man; the same retentive memory; the same keen interest in life, and the same discrimination between things sympathised with and things disapproved of, but there is this very noticeable difference: each of the earlier stories contains a character who more or less closely represents Tolstoy himself, through whose eyes everything is seen. "Hadji Murad," on the contrary, is written quite objectively. Before he wrote it Tolstoy had become sure of himself, and felt that he had only to tell the story, and that his judgment of men and of actions would justify itself without his own point of view even needing to be explicitly stated.

In ''Hadji Murad," as in all his later writings, Tolstoy makes us feel how repugnant to him were the customary ways of the life we call ''civilised," with its selfishness and self-indulgence, its officialism, banquets, balls, and masquerades, and above all, with its complete lack of spiritual fervour. The manners and customs of the semi-savage tribesmen arouse no such abhorrence in him. The natural instinctive spontaneity of their conduct appeals to him; and throughout the tale he makes us feel that Hadji Murad could not possibly have acted otherwise than as he did, either when he deserted the Russians or when he returned to them, or when he slew his guards and tried once more to escape to the mountains. Hadji Murad held life cheap—his own as well as that of other people; but though he spilt much blood, he never arouses the antipathy we are made to feel for the pedantic, stupid cruelty of Nicholas I.

Especially attractive to Tolstoy is the religious fervour of self-abnegation, and the readiness for self-sacrifice in a great cause, which were so frequently shown by the mountaineers.

We are more closely akin to the men of other lands than we often realise; and lest some one reading this book should say to himself, "Yes, the Russians are so-and-so, but we are not as they..." it may be well to mention that the elder Vorontsov's mother was an Englishwoman, a Herbert of the Pembroke family. For that fact, and for much else, I am indebted to Mr. J. F. Baddeley, and especially for his version of the song of the blood-feud sung by Khanefii, which I have borrowed.

The footnotes are not part of the original work, but belong to the translation.

AYLMER MAUDE.

HADJI MURAD[1]

Chapter - I

I was returning home by the fields. It was midsummer, the hay harvest was over and they were just beginning to reap the rye. At that season of the year there is a delightful variety of flowers —red white and pink scented tufty clover; milk-white ox-eye daisies with their bright yellow centres and pleasant spicy smell; yellow honey-scented rape blossoms; tall campanulas with white and lilac bells, tulip-shaped; creeping vetch; yellow, red, and pink scabious; plantains with faintly scented, neatly arranged purple plaintains with blossoms slightly tinged with pink; cornflowers, the newly opened blossoms bright blue in the sunshine but growing paler and redder towards evening or when growing old; and delicate almond-scented dodder flowers. I gathered myself a large nosegay and was going home when I noticed in a ditch, in full bloom, a beautiful thistle plant of the crimson variety, which in our neighborhood they call "Tartar" and carefully avoid when mowing— or, if they do happen to cut it down, throw out from among the grass for fear of pricking their hands. Thinking to pick this thistle and put it in the center of my nosegay, I climbed down into the ditch, and after driving away a velvety bumble-bee that had penetrated deep into one of the flowers and had there fallen sweetly asleep, I set to work to pluck the flower. But this proved a very difficult task. Not only did the stalk prick on every side—even through the handkerchief I wrapped round my hand—but it was so tough that I had to struggle with it for nearly five minutes, breaking the fibers one by one; and when I had at last plucked it, the stalk was all frayed and the flower itself no longer seemed so fresh and beautiful. Moreover, owing to a oarseness and stiffness, it did not seem in place among the delicate blossoms of my nosegay. I threw it away feeling sorry to have vainly destroyed a flower that looked beautiful in its proper place, and I Threw it away

"But what energy and tenacity! With what determination it defended itself, and how dearly it sold its life!" thought I, remembering the effort it had cost me to pluckthe flower. The way home led across black-earth fieldsthat had just been ploughed up. I ascended the dusty path. The ploughed field belonged to a landed proprietor and was so large that on both sides and before me to the top of the hill nothing was visible but evenly furrowed and moist earth. The

---

1. Spelt by the Russians Murat Murad seems the more correct.—Ed.

land was well tilled, and nowhere was there a blade of grass or any kind of plant to be seen; it was all black. "Ah, what a destructive creature is man....How many different plant-lives he destroys to support his own existence!" thought I, involuntarily looking round for some living thing in this lifeless black field. In front of me, to the right of the road I saw some kind of little clump, and drawing nearer I found it was the same kind of thistle as that which I had vainly plucked and thrown away. This "Tartar" plant had three branches. One was broken, and stuck out like the stump of a mutilated arm. Each of the other two bore a flower, once red but now blackened. One stalk was broken and half of it hung down with a soiled flower at its tip. The other, though also soiled with black mud, still stood erect. Evidently a cartwheel had passed over the plant but it had risen again and that was why, though erect, it stood twisted to one side, as if a piece of its body had been torn from it, its bowels had been drawn out, an arm torn off, and one of its eyes plucked out; and yet it stood firm and did not surrender to man, who had destroyed all its brothers around it....

"What energy!" I thought. "Man has conquered everything, and destroyed millions of plants, yet this one won't submit." And I remembered a Caucasian episode of years ago, which I had partly seen myself, partly heard of from eye-witnesses, and in part imagined.

The episode, as it has taken shape in my memory and imagination, was as follows.

** * * *

This happened towards the end of 1851.

On a cold November evening Hadji Murád rode into Makhmet, a hostile Chechen *aoul,*[2] that was filled with the scented smoke of burning *kizyák,*[3] and that lay some fifteen miles from Russian territory· The strained chant of the muezzin had just ceased, and through the clear mountain air, impregnated with *kizyak* smoke, above the lowing of the cattle and the bleating of the sheep that were dispersing among the *sáklya*s[4] (which were crowded together like the cells of honeycomb), could be clearly heard the guttural voices of disputing men, and sounds of women's and children's voices rising from near the fountain below.

This was Hadji Murád Shamil's *naib*,[5] famous for his exploits, who used never to ride out without his banner and was always accompanied by some dozens of *murids*, who caracoled and showed off before him. Now with one *murid* only, wrapped in hood and *búrka*,[6] from under which protruded a rifle,

2. Aoul, Tartar village.
3. Kizyak, fuel made of straw and manure.
4. Saklya, a Caucasian house, clay plastered and often built of earth.
5. Naib, Lieutenant or governor.
6. Burka, a long round frlt cape.

he rode, a fugitive, trying to attract as little attention as possible, and peering with his quick black eyes into the faces of those he met on his way.

When he entered the *aoul,* Hadji Murád did not ride up the road leading to the open square, but turned to the left into a narrow side street; and on reaching the second *sáklya*, which was cut into the hillside, he stopped and looked round. There was no one under the penthouse in front; but on the roof of the *sáklya* itself, behind the freshly-plastered clay chimney, lay a man covered with a sheepskin. Hadji Murád touched him with the handle of his leatherplaited whip, and clicked his tongue. An old man rose from under the sheepskin. He had on a greasy old *beshémt*[7] and a nightcap. His moist red eyelids had no lashes, and he blinked to get them unstuck. Hadji Murád, repeating the customary *"Selaam aleikum!"* uncovered his face. *"Aleikum, selaam!"* said the old man, recognising Hadji Murád and smiling with his toothless mouth; and rising up on his thin legs, he began thrusting his feet into the wooden-heeled slippers that stood by the chimney. Then he leisurely slipped his arms into the sleeves of his crumpled sheepskin, and going to the ladder that leant against the roof, he descended backwards. 'While he dressed, and as lie climbed down, he kept shaking his head on its thin, shrivelled sunburnt neck, and mumbling something with his toothless mouth. As soon as he reached the ground he hospitably seized Hadji Murád's bridle and right stirrup; but the strong active *murid* who accompanied Hadji Murád had quickly dismounted and motioning the old man aside, took his place. Hadji Murád also dismounted and, walking with a slight limp, entered under the penthouse. A boy of fifteen, coming quickly out of the door, met him and wonderingly fixed his sparkling eyes, black as ripe sloes, on the new arrivals.

"Run to the mosque and call your father," ordered the old man, as he hurried forward to open the thin, creaking door into the *sáklya*. for Hadji Murád

As Hadji Murád entered the outer door, a slight, spare, middle-aged woman in a yellow smock, red *beshmet*, and wide blue trousers came through an inner door carrying cushions.

"May thy coming bring happiness!" said she, and bending nearly double began arranging the cushions along the front wall for the guest to sit on.

"May thy sons live!" answered Hadji Murád, taking off his *búrka*, his rifle, and his sword and handing them to the old man, who carefully hung the rifle and sword on a nail beside the weapons of the master of the house, which were suspended between two large basins that glittered against the clean clay-plastered and carefully whitewashed wall.

Hadji Murád adjusted the pistol at his back, came up to the cushions and wrapping his Circassian coat closer round him, sat down. The old man squatted on his bare heels beside him, closed his eyes, and lifted his hands, palms upwards. Hadji Murád did the same; then, after repeating a prayer they both

7. Beshmet, a Tartar undergarment with sleeves.

stroked their faces, passing their hands downwards till the palms joined at the end of their beards.

"Ne habar?" asked Hadji Murád, addressing the old man. (That is, "Is There anything new?")

"Habar yok" ("Nothing new"), replied the old man, looking with his lifeless red eyes not at Hadji Murád's face but at his breast. "I live at the apiary and have only to-day come to see my son....He knows."

Hadji Murád, understanding that the old man did not wish to say what he knew and what Hadji Murád wanted to know, slightly nodded his head and asked no more questions.

"There is no good news," said the old man. "The only news is that the hares keep discussing how to drive away the eagles and the eagles tear first one and then another of them. The other day the Russian dogs burnt the hay in the Mitchit *aoul*....May their faces be torn!" added he hoarsely and angrily.

Hadji Murád's *murid* entered the room, his strong legs striding softly over the earthen floor. Retaining only his dagger and pistol, he shook off his *búrka*, rifle, and sword as Hadji Murád had done, and hung them up on the same nails as his leader's weapons.

"Who is he?" asked the old man, pointing to the newcomer.

"My *murid.* Eldár is his name," said Hadji Murád.

"That is well," said the old man, and motioned Eldár to a place on a piece of felt beside Hadji Murád. Eldár sat down, crossing his legs and fixing his fine ram-like eyes on the old man who, having now started talking, was telling how their brave fellows had caught two Russian soldiers the week before and had killed one and sent the other to Shamil in Veden.

Hadji Murád heard him absently, looking at the door and listening to the sounds outside. Under the penthouse steps were heard, the door creaked, and Sado, the master of the house, came in. He was a man of about forty, with a small beard, long nose, and eyes as black, though not as glittering, as those of his fifteen-year-old son who had run to call him home, and who now entered with his father and sat down by the door. The master of the house took off his wooden slippers at the door, and pushing his old and much-worn cap on to the back of his head (which had remained unshaved so long that it was beginning to be overgrown with black hair), at once squatted down in front of Hadji Murád.

He too lifted his hands, palms upwards, as the old man had done, repeated a prayer, and then stroked his face downwards. Only after that did he begin to speak. He told how an order had come from Shamil to seize Hadji Murád, alive or dead; that Shamil's envoys had left only the day before; that the people were afraid to disobey Shamil's orders; and that therefore it was necessary to be careful.

8. Kunak sworn friend guest.

"In my house," said Sado, "no one shall injure my *kunak*[8] while I live; but how will it be in the open fields?...We must think it over."

Hadji Murád listened with attention and nodded approvingly. When Sado had finished he said,—

"Very well. Now we must send a man with a letter to the Russians. My *murid* will go, but he will need a guide."

"I will send brother Bata," said Sado. "Go and call Bata," he added, turning to his son.

The boy instantly bounded to his nimble feet as if he were on springs, and swinging his arms, rapidly left the *sáklya*. Some ten minutes later he returned with a sinewy, short-legged Chechen, burnt almost black by the sun, wearing a worn and tattered yellow Circassian coat with frayed sleeves, and crumpled black leggings.

Hadji Murád greeted the newcomer, and at once, and again without wasting a single word, immediately asked,—

"Canst thou conduct my *murid* to the Russians?"

"I can," gaily replied Bata. "I can certainly do it. There is not another Chechen who would pass as I can. Another might agree to go, and might promise anything, but would do nothing; but I can do it!"

"All right," said Hadji Murád. "Thou wilt receive three for thy trouble," and he held up three fingers.

Bata nodded to show that he understood, and added that it was not money he prized, but that he was ready to serve Hadji Murád for the honour alone. Every one in the mountains knew Hadji Murád, and how he slew the Russian swine.

"Very well....A rope should be long, but a speech short," said Hadji Murád.

"Well then I'll hold my tongue," said Bata.

"Where the river Argun bends by the cliff," said Hadji Murád, "there are two stacks in a glade in the forest— thou knowest?"

"I know."

"There my four horsemen are waiting for me," said Hadji Murád.

"Aye," answered Bata, nodding.

"Ask for Khan Mahoma. He knows what to do and what to say. Canst thou lead him to the Russian Commander, Prince Vorontsóv?"

"I'll take him There."

"Take him, and bring him back again. Canst thou?"

"I can."

"Take him there and return to the wood. I shall be there too."

"I will do it all," said Bata, rising, and putting his hands on his heart he went out.

Hadji Murád turned to his host when Bata had gone.

"A man must also be sent to Chekhi," he began, and took hold of one of the cartridge pouches of his Circassian coat, but immediately let his hand drop and became silent on seeing two women enter the *sáklya.*

One was Sado's wife—the thin middle-aged woman who had arranged the cushions for Hadji Murád. The other was quite a young girl, wearing red trousers and a green *beshmét;* A necklace of silver coins covered the whole front of her dress, and at the end of the not long but thick plait of hard black hair that hung between her thin shoulder-blades a silver ruble was suspended. Her eyes, as sloe-black as those of her father and brother, sparkled brightly in her young face, which tried to be stern. She did not look at the visitors, but evidently felt their presence.

Sado's wife brought in a low round table, on which stood tea, pancakes in butter, cheese, *churek* (that is, thinly rolled out bread), and honey. The girl carried a basin, a ewer, and a towel.

Sado and Hadji Murád kept silent as long as the women, with their coin ornaments tinkling, moved softly about in their red soft-soled slippers, setting out before the visitors the things they had brought. Eldár sat motionless as a statue, his ram-like eyes fixed on his crossed legs, all the time the women were in the *sáklya*. Only after they had gone, and their soft footsteps could no longer be heard behind the door, did he give a sigh of relief.

Hadji Murád having pulled out a pulled out a bullet that plugged one of the bullet-pouches of his Circassian coat, and having taken out a rolled-up note that lay beneath it, held it out, saying:

"To be handed to my son."

"Where must the answer be sent?"

"To thee and thou must forward it to me."

"It shall be done," said Sado, and placed the note in a cartridge-pocket of his own coat. Then he took up the metal ewer and moved the basin towards Hadji Murád.

Hadji Murád turned up the sleeves of his *beshmét* on his white muscular arms, and held out his hands under the clear cold water which Sado poured from the ewer. Having wiped them on a clean unbleached towel, Hadji Murád turned to the table. Eldár did the same. While the visitors ate, Sado sat opposite, and thanked them several times for their visit. The boy sat by the door never taking his sparkling eyes off Hadji Murád's face, and smiled as if in confirmation of his father's words.

Though Hadji Murád had eaten nothing for more than twenty-four hours he ate only a little bread and cheese; then, drawing out a small knife from under his dagger, he spread some honey on a piece of bread.

"Our honey is good," said the old man, evidently pleased to see Hadji Murád eating his honey. "This year, above all other years, it is plentiful and good."

"I thank thee," said Hadji Murád, and turned from the table. Eldár would have liked to go on eating, but he followed his leader's example, and having moved away from the table, handed Hadji Murád the ewer and basin.

Sado knew that he was risking his life by receiving Hadji Murád in his house, after his quarrel with Shamil the latter had issued a proclamation to all the inhabitants of Chechnya forbidding them to receive Hadji Murád on pain of death. He knew that the inhabitants of the *aoul* might at any moment become aware of Hadji Murád's presence in his house, and might demand his surrender; but this not only did not frighten Sado, but even gave him pleasure with himself because he was doing his duty.

"Whilst thou art in my house and my head is on my shoulders no one shall harm thee," he repeated to Hadji Murád.

Hadji Murád looked into his glittering eyes and understanding that this was true, said with some solemnity,—

"Mayest thou receive joy and life!"

Sado silently laid his hand on his heart as a sign of thanks for these kind words.

Having closed the shutters of the *sáklya* and laid some sticks in the fireplace, Sado, in an exceptionally bright and animated mood, left the room and went into that part of his *sáklya* where his family all lived. The women had not yet gone to sleep, and were talking about the dangerous visitors who were spending the night in their guest chambers.

CHAPTER II

At the advanced fort Vozdvizhensk, situated some ten miles from the *aoul* in which Hadji Murád was spending the night, three soldiers and a non-commissioned officer left the fortification and went beyond the Shahgirinsk Gate. The soldiers, dressed as Caucasian soldiers used to be in those days, wore sheepskin coats and caps, and boots that reached above their knees, and they carried their cloaks tightly rolled up and fastened across their shoulders. Shouldering arms, they first went some five hundred paces along the road, and then turned off it and went some twenty paces to the right—the dead leaves rustling under their boots—till they reached the blackened trunk of a broken plane tree, just visible through the darkness. There they stopped. It was at this plane tree that an ambush party was usually placed.

The bright stars, that seemed to be running along the tree-tops while the soldiers were walking through the forest, now stood still, shining brightly between the bare branches of the trees.

"A good job it's dry," said the non-commissioned officer, Panóv, bringing down his long gun and bayonet with a clang from his shoulder, and placing it against the plane tree. The three soldiers did the same.

"Sure enough, I've lost it!" crossly muttered Panóv. "Must have left it behind, or I've dropped it on the way."

"What are you looking for?" asked one of the soldiers in a bright, cheerful voice.

"The bowl of my pipe. Where the devil has it got to?"

"Have you got the stem?" asked the cheerful voice.

"Here's the stem".

"Then why not stick it straight into the ground?"

"Not worth bothering!"

"We'll manage that in a minute."

It was forbidden to smoke in while in ambush, but this ambush hardly deserved the name. It was rather an outpost to prevent the mountaineers from bringing up a cannon unobserved and firing at the fort as they used to do. Panóv did not consider it necessary to forego the pleasure of smoking, and therefore accepted the cheerful soldier's offer. The latter took a knife from his pocket and dug with it a hole in the ground. Having smoothed this round, he adjusted the pipe stem to it, then filled the hole with tobacco and pressed it down, and the pipe was ready. A sulphur match flared and for a moment lit up the broad-cheeked face of the soldier who lay on his stomach, the air whistled in the stem, and Panóv smelt the pleasant odour of burning tobacco.

"Fixed it up?" said he, rising to his feet.

"Why, of course!"

"What a smart chap you are, Avdéev!...As wise as a judge! Now then, lad." Avdéev rolled over on his side to make room for Panóv, letting smoke escape from his mouth.

Panóv lay down prone, and after wiping the mouthpiece with his sleeve, began to inhale.

When they had their smoke the soldiers began to talk.

"They say the commander has had his fingers in the cash-box again," remarked one of them in a lazy voice. "He lost at cards, you see."

"He'll pay it back again," said Panóv.

"Of course he will! He's a good officer," assented Avdéev.

"Good! good!" gloomily repeated the man who had started the conversation. "In my opinion the company ought to speak to him. 'If you've taken the money, tell us how much and when you'll repay it.'"

"That will be as the company decides," said Panóv, tearing himself away from the pipe.

"Of course. 'The community is a strong man,'" assented Avdéev, quoting a proverb.

"There will be oats to buy and boots to get towards spring. The money will be wanted, and shall we do what if he's pocketed it?" insisted the dissatisfied one.

"I tell you it will be as the company wishes," repeated Panóv. "It's not the first time: he takes, and gives back."

In the Caucasus in those days each company chose men to manage its own commissariat. They received 6 rubles 50 kopeks a month per man[1] from the treasury, and catered for the company. They planted cabbages, made hay, had their own carts, and prided themselves on their well-fed horses. The company's money was kept in a chest of which the commander had the key: and it often happened that he borrowed from the chest. This had just happened again, and that was what the soldiers were talking about. The morose soldier, Nikitin, wished to demand an account from the commander, while Panóv and Avdéev considered that unnecessary.

After Panóv, Nikitin had a smoke; and then, spreading his cloak on the ground sat down on it leaning against the trunk of the plane tree. The soldiers were silent. Only far above their heads the crowns of the trees rustled in the

---

1. About E1. for at that time the rouble was worth about three shillings.

wind Suddenly, above this incessant low rustling, rose the howling, whining, weeping and chuckling of jackals.

"Hear those accursed creatures—how they caterwaul!"

"They're laughing at you because your mug's all on one side," remarked the high voice of another soldier, a Litte Russian.

All was silent again: only the wind swayed the branches, now revealing and now hiding the stars.

"I say, Panóv," suddenly asked the cheerful Avdéev, "do you ever feel dull?"

"Dull, why?" replied Panóv reluctantly.

"Well, I do feel dull… dull sometimes that I don't know what I might not be ready to do to myself."

"There now!" was all Panóv replied.

"That time when I drank all the money, it was from dullness. It took hold of me…took hold of me till I think to myself, 'I'll just get blind drunk!'"

"But sometimes drinking makes it still worse."

"Yes, that's happened to me too. But what is one to do with himself?"

"But what makes you feel so dull?"

"What, me?…Why, it's the longing for home."

"Is yours a wealthy home, then?"

"No, we weren't wealthy, but things went properly—we lived well." And Avdéev began to relate what he had already many times told to Panóv.

"You see, I went as a soldier of my own free will, instead of my brother," he said. "He has children. They were five in family, and I had only just married. Mother began begging me to go. So I thought, 'Well, maybe they will remember what I've done.' So I went to our proprietor…he was a good master and he said, 'You're a fine fellow, go!' So I went instead of my brother."

"Well, that was right," said Panóv.

"And yet, will you believe me, Panóv, if I now feel so dull, it's chiefly because of that? 'Why did you go instead of your brother?' I say. 'He's now living like a king over there, while I have to suffer here;' and the more I think the worse I fell…Seems it's just a piece of ill-luck!"

Avdéev was silent.

"Perhaps we'd better have another smoke," said he after a pause.

"Well then, fix it up!"

But the soldiers were not to have their smoke. Hardly had Avdéev risen to fix the pipe stem in its place when above the rustling of the trees they heard footsteps along the road. Panóv took his gun, and pushed Nikitin with his foot.

Nikitin rose and picked up his cloak.

The third soldier, Bondarenko, rose also, and said,—

"And I have dreamt such a dream, mates...."

"Sh!" said Avdeev, and the soldiers held their breath, listening. The footsteps of men not shod in hard boots were heard approaching. Clearer and clearer through the darkness was heard a rustling of the fallen leaves and dry twigs. Then came the peculiar guttural tones of Chechen voices. The soldiers now not only heard, but saw two shadows passing through a clear space between the trees. One shadow was taller than the other. When these shadows had come in line with the soldiers, Panov, gun in hand, stepped out on to the road, followed by his comrades.

"Who goes there?" cried he.

"Me, friendly Chechen," said the shorter one. This was Bata. "Gun, yok![2]...sword, yok!" said he, pointing to himself. "Prince, want!"

The taller one stood silent beside his comrade. He, too was unarmed.

"He means he's a scout, and wants the Colonel," explained Panóv to his comrades.

"Prince Vorontsóv...much want! Big business!" said Bata.

"All right, all right! We'll take you to him," said Panóv. "I say, you'd better take them," said he to Avdéev, "you and Bondarenko; and when you've given them up to the officer on duty come back again. Mind," he added, "be careful to make them keep in front of you!"

"And what of this?" said Avdéev, moving his gun and bayonet as though stabbing someone. "I'd just give a dig, and let the steam out of him!"

"What'll he be worth when you've stuck him?" remarked Bondarenko.

"Now, march!"

When the steps of the two soldiers conducting the scouts could no longer be heard, Panóv and Nikitin returned to their post.

"What the devil brings them here at night?" said Nikitin.

"Seems it's necessary," said panov. "But it's getting chilly," he added, and unrolling his cloak he put it on and sat down by the tree.

About two hours later Avdéev and Bondarenko returned.

"Well, have you handed them over?"

"Yes. They're'not yet asleep at the Colonel's—they were taken straight in to him. And do you know, mates, those shaven-headed lads are fine!" continued Avdéev. "Yes, really. What a talk I had with them!"

"Of course you'd talk," remarked Nikitin disapprovingly.

"Really they're just like Russians. One of them is married. 'Molly,' says I, 'bar?'[3] 'Bar,' he says. Bondarenko, didn't I say 'bar?' 'Many bar?' 'A couple,' says he. A couple! Such a good talk we had! Such nice fellows!"

---

2. Yok, on not.

3. Bar, have.

"Nice, indeed!" said Nikitin. "If you met him alone he'd soon let the guts out of you."

"It will be getting light before long." said panov.

"Yes, the stars are beginning to go out," said Avdéev, sitting down and making himself comfortable.

And the soldiers were silent again.

CHAPTER III

The windows of the barracks and of the soldiers' houses had long been dark in the fort; but there were still light in the windows of the best hous there.

In it lived Prince Simon Mikhailovich Vorontsóv, Commander of the Kurín Regiment, an imperial aide-de-camp and son of the Commander-in-Chief. Vorontsóv's lived with his wife, Marya Vasilevna, a famous Petersburg beauty, and lived in this little Caucasian fort more luxuriously than any one had ever lived there before. To Vorontsóv, and especially to his wife, it seemed that they were not only living a very modest life, but one full of privations; while to the inhabitants of the place their luxury was surprising and extraordinary.

Now at midnight, in the spacious drawing-room with its carpeted floor, its rich curtains drawn across the windows, at a card table lit by four candles, sat the hosts and their visitors, playing cards. One of the players was Vorontsov himself: a long-faced, fair-haired colonel, wearing the initials and gold cords of an aide-de-camp. His partner—a graduate of Petersburg University, whom the Princess Vorontsov had lately had sent out as tutor to her little son (born of her first marriage)—was a shaggy young man of gloomy appearance. Against them played two officers: one a broad and red-faced man, Poltorátsky, a company commander, who had exchanged out of the guards ; and the other, the regimental adjutant, a man with a cold expression on his handsome face, who sat very straight on his chair.

The Princess Mary Vasilevna, the large-built, large-eyed, black-browed beauty, sat beside Poltorátsky (her crinoline touching his legs—and looked over his cards. In her words, her looks, and her smile, in her perfume, and in every movement of her body, there was something that reduced Poltorátsky to obliviousness of everything except the consciousness of her nearness, and he made blunder after blunder, trying his partner's temper more and more.

"No…that's too bad! You've again wasted an ace," said the regimental adjutant, flushing all over, as Poltorátsky threw out an ace.

Poltorátsky uncomprehendingly—as though he had just awoke—turned his kindly, wide-set black eyes towards the dissatisfied Adjutant.

"Do forgive him!" said Mary Vasilevna, smiling. "There, you see! Didn't I tell you so?" she went on, turning to Poltorátsky.

"But that's not at all what you said," replied Poltorátsky, smiling.

"Wasn't it?" she replied, also smiling; and this answering smile excited and delighted Poltorátsky to such a degree that he blushed crimson, and seizing the cards began to shuffle.

"It isn't your turn to deal," said the Adjutant sternly, and with his white ringed hand he himself began to deal, as though he wished to get rid of the cards as quickly as possible.

The prince's valet entered the drawing-room and announced that the officer on duty wanted the prince.

"Excuse me, gentlemen," said the prince, speaking Russian with an English accent. "Will you take my place, marie?"

"Do you all agree?" asked the princess, rising quickly and lightly to her full height, rustling her silks, and smiling the radiant smile of a happy woman.

"I always agree to everything," replied the Adjutant, very pleased that the princess—who could not play at all—was now going to play against him.

Poltorátsky only spread out his hands and smiled.

The rubber was nearly finished when the prince returned to the drawing-room. He came back animated and very pleased.

"Do you know what I propose?"

"What is it?"

"Let us have some champagne."

"I am always ready for that," said Poltorátsky.

"Why not? We shall be delighted!" said the Adjutant.

"Vasily! bring some," said the Prince.

"What did they want you for?" asked Mary Vasilevna.

"It was the officer on duty and another man."

"Who? What about?" asked Marya Vasilevna quickly.

"I mustn't say," said Vorontsóv, shrugging his shoulders.

"You mustn't say!" repeated Marya Vasilevna. "We'll" see about that."

When the champagne was brought, each of the visitors drank a glass and having finished the game and settled the scores they began to take their leave.

"Is it your company that's ordered to the forest to-morrow?" the prince asked Poltorátsky as they said goodbye.

"Yes, mine…why?"

"Oh, then we'll meet to-morrow," said the prince, slightly smiling .

"Very pleased," replied Poltorátsky, not quite understanding what Vorontsóv was saying to him, and preoccupied only by the thought that he would in a minute be pressing Mary Vasilevna's hand.

Marya Vasilevna, according to her wont, not only firmly pressed his hand but shook it vigorously, and again reminding him of his mistake in playing dia monds, she gave him what to Poltoratšky to be a delightful, affectionate, and meaning smile.

Poltorátsky went home in an ecstatic condition only to be understood by people like himself who, having grown up and been educated in society, meet a woman belonging to their own circle after months of isolated military life, and moreover a woman like Princess Vorontsóv.

When he reached the little house in which he and his comrade lived he pushed the door, but it was locked. He knocked, but still the door was not opened. He felt vexed, and began banging the door with his foot and his sword. Then he heard a sound of footsteps, and Vovilo — a domestic serf belonging to Poltorátsky — undid the cabin-hook which fastened the door.

"What do you mean by locking yourself in, blockhead?"

"But how is it possible, sir...?"

"You're tipsy again! I'll show you 'how it is possible!'" and Poltorátsky was about to strike Vovilo but changed his mind. "Well, go to the devil! ... Light a candle."

"In a minute."

Vovílo had been taken "up" when a boy; that is, he had been taken into his owner's household service; and now he was already over forty, was not married, and lived a campaigning life with his harum-scarum young master. He was a good master, who seldom struck him; but what kind of a life was it? ''He promised to free me when we return from the Caucasus, but where am I to go with my freedom?...It's a dog's life!" thought Vovilo; and he felt so sleepy that, afraid lest some one should come in and steal something, he fastened the hook of the door and fell asleep.

* * * *

Plotorátsky entered the bedroom which he shared with his comrade Tíkhonof.

"Well, have you lost?" asked Tikhonof, waking up.

"As it happens, I haven't. I've won seventeen rubles, and we drank a bottle of Cliquot!"

"And you've looked at Mary Vasilevna?"

"Yes, and I have looked at Mary Vasilevna," repeated Poltorátsky.

"It will soon be time to get up," said Tikhonof. "We are to start at six."

"Vovilo!" shouted Poltorátsky, "see that you wake me up properly to-morrow at five!"

"How's one to wake you if you fight?"

"I tell you you're to wake me! Do you hear?"

"All right." Vovílo went out, taking Poltorátsky's boots and clothes with him. Poltorátsky got into bed, and smoked a cigarette and put out his candle. In the dark he saw before him the smiling face of Marya Vasilevna.

* * * *

The Vorontsóvs did not go to bed at once. When the visitors had left, Mary Vasílevna went up to her husband, and standing in front of him, said severely,—

"Eh bien! vous allez me dire ce que c'est."[1]

"Mais, ma chere..."

"Pas de 'ma chere'! C'etait un emissaire, n'est-ce pas?"

"Quand meme, je ne puis pas vous le dire."

"Vous ne pouvez pas? Alors, c'est moi qui vais vous le dire!"

"Vous?"

"It was Hadji Murád, wasn't it?" said Mary Vasilevna, who had for some days past heard of the negotiations, and thought that Hadji Murád himself had been to see her husband. Vorontsóv could not altogether deny this, but disappointed her by saying that it was not Hadji Murád himself but only an emissary to announce that Hadji Murád would come to meet him next day at the spot where a wood-cutting expedition had been arranged.

In the monotonous life of the fortress, the young Vorontsóvs—both husband and wife—were glad of this occurrence; and when, after speaking of the pleasure the news would give his father, they went to bed, it was already past two o'clock.

---

1. "Well now ! You're going to tell me it's all about...."
"But my dear..."
"Don'tmy dear me ! It was an emissary, wasn't it?"
"Well supposing it was still I must not tell you"
"You must not Well then It's I who will tell you ..."
"You?"

CHAPTER IV

After the three sleepless nights he had passed flying from the *murids* Shamil sent to capture him, Hadji Murád fell asleep as soon as Sado, having bid him good-night, had gone out of the *sáklya*. He slept fully dressed with his head on his hand, his elbow sinking deep into the red down-cushions his host had arranged for him.

At a little distance, by the wall, slept Eldár. He lay on his back, his strong young limbs stretched out so that his high chest with the black cartridge-pouches sewn into the front of his white Circassian coat was higher than his freshly-shaven, blue-gleaming head, which had rolled off the pillow and was thrown back. His upper lip, on which a little soft down was just appearing, pouted like a child's, now contracting and now expanding, as though he were sipping something. He, like Hadji Murád slept with pistol and dagger in his belt. The sticks in the grate burnt low, and a nightlight in a niche in the wall gleamed faintly.

In the middle of the night the floor of the guest-chamber creaked, and Hadji Murád immediately rose, putting his hand to his pistol. Sado entered, treading softly on the earthen floor.

"What is it?" asked Hadji Murád, as if he had not been asleep at all.

"We must think," replied Sado, squatting down in front of him. "A woman from her roof saw you arrive and told her husband; and now the whole *aoul* knows. A neighbor, has just been to tell my wife that the Elders have assembled in the mosque, and want to detain you."

"I must be off!" said Hadji Murád.

"The horses are saddled," said Sado, quickly leaving the *sáklya.*

"Eldár!" whispered Hadji Murád. And Eldár, hearing his name, and above all his master's voice, leapt to his feet, setting straight his cap.

Hadji Murád donned his weapons and then his *búrka*. Eldár did the same, and they both went silently out of the *sáklya* into the penthouse. The black-eyed boy brought their horses. Hearing the clatter of hoofs on the hard-beaten road, someone stuck his head out of the door of a neighbouring *sáklya* and a man ran up the hill towards the mosque. There was no moon, but the stars shone brightly in the black *sáklya* that the outlines of the sdklya roofs could be seen in the darkness, and rising above the other buildings, the mosque with its minarets in the upper part of the village. From the mosque came a hum of voices.

Hadji Murád quickly seizing his gun, placed his foot in the narrow stirrup, and silently and easily throwing his body across, swung himself on to the high cushion of the saddle.

"May God reward you!" he said, addressing his host while his right foot felt instinctively for the stirrup, and with his whip he lightly touched the lad who held his horse, as a sign that he should let go. The boy stepped aside; and the horse, as if it knew what it had to do, started at a brisk pace down the lane towards the principal street. Eldár rode behind him. Sado in his sheepskin followed, almost running, swinging his arms, and crossing now to one side and now to the other of the narrow side-street. At the place where the streets met, first one moving shadow and then another appeared in the road.

"Stop…who's that? Stop!" shouted a voice, and several men blocked the path.

Instead of stopping, Hadji Murád drew his pistol from his belt, and increasing his speed rode straight at those who blocked the way. They separated, and Hadji Murád without looking round started down the road at a swift canter. Eldár followed him at a sharp trot. Two shots cracked behind them, and two bullets whistled past without hitting either Hadji Murád or Eldár. Hadji Murád continued riding at the same pace, but having gone some three hundred yards, he stopped his slightly panting horse, and listened.

In front of him, lower down, gurgled rapidly running water. Behind him, in the *aoul* cocks crowed, answering one another. Above these sounds he heard behind him the approaching tramp of horses, and the voices of several men. Hadji Murád touched his horse and rode on at an even pace. Those behind him galloped and soon overtook him. They were some twenty mounted men, inhabitants of the *aoul,* who had decided to detain Hadji Murád or at least to make a show of detaining him in order to justify themselves in Shamil's eyes. When they came near enough to be seen in the darkness, Hadji Murád stopped, let go his bridle, and with an accustomed movement of his of his left hand unbuttoned the cover of his rifle, which he drew forth with his right. Eldár did the same.

"What do you want?" cried Hadji Murád. "Do you wish to take me?"… Take me, then!" and he raised his rifle. The men form the aoul stopped, and Hadji Murád, rifle in hand, rode down into the ravine. The mounted men followed him but did not draw any nearer. When Hadji Murád had crossed to the other side of the ravine, the men shouted to him that he should hear what they had to say. In reply he fired his rifle and put his horse to a gallop. When he reined it in, his pursuers were no longer within hearing, and the crowing of the cocks could also no longer be heard; only the murmur of the water in the forest sounded more distinctly, and now and then came the cry of an owl. The black wall of the forest appeared quite close. It was in the forest that his *murids* awaited him.

On reaching it Hadji Murád paused, and drawing much air into his lungs he whistled and then listened silently. The next minute he was answered by a similar whistle from the forest. Hadji Murád turned from the road and entered it. When he had gone about a hundred paces, he saw among the trunks of the trees a bonfire, the shadows of some men sitting round it, and, half lit-up by the firelight, a hobbled horse which was saddled. Four men were sitting by the fire.

One of them rose quickly, and coming up to Hadji Murád took hold of his bridle and stirrup. This was Hadji Murád's sworn brother who managed his household affairs for him.

"Put out the fire," said Hadji Murád, dismounting.

The men began scattering the pile, and trampling on the burning branches.

"Has Bata been here?" asked Hadji Murád, moving towards a *búrka* that was spread on the ground.

"Yes, he went away long ago with Khan Mahomá."

"Which way did they go?"

"That way," answered Khanefi pointing in the opposite direction to that from which Hadji Murád had come.

"All right," said Hadji Murád, and unslinging his rifle he began to load it.

"We must take care—I have been pursued," he said to a man who was putting out the fire.

He was Gamzálo, a Chechen. Gamzálo approached the *barka*, took up a rifle that lay on it wrapped in its cover, and without a word went to that side of the glade from which Hadji Murád had come.

Eldár, When he had dismounted he took Hadji Murád's horse, and having reined up both horses heads high, tied them to two trees. Then he shouldered his rifle, as Gamzálo had done, and went to the other side of the glade. The bonfire was extinguished, the forest no longer looked so black as before, and in the sky the stars shone, though but faintly.

Lifting his eyes to the stars, and seeing that the Pleiades had already risen half-way up the sky, Hadji Murád calculated that it must be long past midnight and that his nightly prayer was long overdue. He asked Khanefi for a ewer (they always carried one in their packs), and putting on his *barka* he went to the water.

Having taken off his shoes and performed his ablutions, Hadji Murád stepped on to the *búrka* with bare feet, and then squatted down on his calves, and having first placed his fingers in his ears and closed his eyes, he turned to the *south and recited the usual prayer.*

When he had finished he returned to the place where the saddle-bags lay, and sitting down on the *búrka* he leant his elbows on his knees and bowed his head, and fell into deep thought.

Hadji Murád always had great faith in his own fortune. When planning anything he always felt in advance firmly convinced of success, and fate smiled on him. It was so, with a few rare exceptions, during the whole course of his stormy militray life; and so he hoped it would be now. He pictured to himself how—with the army vorontsov would place at his disposal— he would march against Shamil and take him prisoner, and revenge himself on him; and how the Russian Tsar would reward him, and how he would again rule over not only Avaria, but over the whole of Chechnya, which would submit to him. With these thoughts he fell asleep befome he was aware of it.

He dreamt how he and his brave followers rushed at Shamil with songs and with the cry, "Hadji Murád is coming!" and how they seized him and his wives and he heard the wives crying and sobbing. He woke up. The song, *Lya-il-allysha,* and the cry "Hadji Murád is coming!" and the weeping of shamil's wives, was the howling, weeping and laughter of jackals that awoke him. Hadji Murád lifted his head, glanced at the sky which seen between the trunks of the trees, was already getting light in the east, and inquired after Khan Mahoma of a *murid* who sat at some distance from him. On hearing that Khan Mahoma had not yet returned, Hadji Murád again bowed his head and fell asleep at once.

He was awakened by the merry voice of Khan Mahoma, returning from his mission with Bata. Khan Mahoma at once sat down beside Hadji Murád, and told him how the soldiers had met them and had led them to the prince himself and how pleased the prince was, and how he promised to meet them in the morning; where the Russians would be felling trees beyond the Mitchik drums in the Shalin glade. Bata interrupted his fellow- envoy to add details of his own.

Hadji Murád asked particularly for the words with which Vorontsóv had answered his offer to go over to the Russians; and Khan Mahoma and Bata replied with one voice that the prince promised to receive Hadji Murád as a guest, and to act so that it should be well for him.

Then Hadji Murád questioned them about the road, and when Khan Mahoma assured him that he knew the way well and would conduct him straight to the spot, Hadji Murád took out some money and gave Bata the promised three rubles; and he ordered his men to take out of the saddle bags his gold-ornamented weapons and his turban, and to clean themselves up so as to look well when they arrived among the Russians.

While they cleaned their weapons, harness and horses, the stars faded away; it became quite light, and an early morning breeze sprang up.

CHAPTER V

Early in the morning, while it was still dark, two companies, carrying axes and commanded by Poltorátsky marched six miles beyond the Shagirinsk Gate, and having thrown out a line of sharpshooters, set to work to fell trees as soon as the day broke. Towards eight o'clock the mist which had mingled with the perfumed smoke of the hissing and crackling damp green branches on the bonfires began to rise, and the wood-fellers—who till then had not seen five paces off, but had only heard one another—began to see both the bonfires and the road through the forest, blocked with falled trees. The sun now appeared like a bright spot in the fog, and now again was hidden.

In the glade, some way from the road, Poltorátsky, and his subaltern Tikhonov, two officers of the 3rd Company, and Baron Freze, an ex-officer of the Guards who had been reduced to the ranks for a duel, a fellow-student of Poltoratsky 's at the Cadet College, were sites ting on drums. Bits of paper that had contained food, cigarette stumps, and empty bottles lay scattered round the drums. The officers had had some vodka, and were now eating,and drinking porter. A drummer was uncorking their third bottle.

Poltorátsky, although he had not had enough sleep, was in that peculiar state of elation and kindly careless gaiety which he always felt when he found himself among his soldiers and with his comrades, where there was a possibility of danger.

The officers were carrying on an animated conversation, the subject of which was the latest news: the death of General Sleptsov. None of them saw in this death that most important moment of a life—its termination and return to the source when it sprang—but they only saw in it the valour of a gallant officer, who rushed at the mountaineers sword in hand and desperately hacked them.

Though all of them—and especially those who had been in action—knew and could not help knowing that never in those days in the Caucasus, nor in fact anywhere, nor at any time did such hand-to-hand hacking as is always imagined and described take place (or if hacking with swords and bayonets ever does take place, it is only those who are running away that get hacked), that fiction of hand-to-hand fighting endowed them with the calm pride and cheerfulness with which they sat on drums (some with a jaunty air, others on the contrary in a very modest pose), drank and joked without troubling about death, which might overtake them at any moment as it had overtaken Sleptsov.

And, as if to confirm their expectations, in the midst of their talk, they heard to the left of the road the pleasing stirring sound of a rifle-shot; and a bullet, merrily whistling somewhere in the misty air, flew past and crashed into a tree.

"Hullo!" exclaimed Poltorátsky in a merry voice; "Why that's at our line. … There now, Kostya," and he turned to Freze, "now's your chance. Go back to the company. I will lead the whole company to support the cordon, and we'll arrange a battle that will be simply delightful … and then we'll make a report.

"Freze jumped to his feet and went at a quick pace towards the smoke-enveloped spot where he had left his company.

Poltorátsky's little Kabarda dapple-bay was brought to him, and he mounted and drew up his company, and led it in the direction whence the shots were fired. The outposts stood on the skirts of the forest, in front of the bare descending slope of a ravine. The wind was blowing in the direction of the forest, and not only was it possible to see the slope of the ravine, but the opposite side of it was also distinctly visible. When Poltorátsky rode up to the line, the sun came out from behind the mist; and on the other side of the ravine, by the outskirts of a young forest, a few horsemen could be seen at a distance of a quarter of a mile, a few horsemen became visible. They were the Chechens who had pursued Hadji Murád and wanted to see him meet the Russians. One of them fired at the line. Several soldiers fired back. The Chechens retreated, and the firing ceased.

But when Poltorátsky and his company came up he nevertheles gave orders to fire; and scarcely had the word been passed, when along the whole line of sharpshooters started the incessant, merry, stirring rattle of our rifles, acompanied by pretty dissolving cloudlets of smoke. The soldiers, pleased to have some distraction, hastened to load, and fired shot after shot. The Chechens evidently caught the feeling of excitement, and leaping forward one after another, fired a few shots at our men. One of these shots wounded a soldier. It was the same Avdéev who had lain in ambush the night before.

When his comrades approached him he was lying prone, holding his wounded stomach with both hands, and rocking himself with a rhythmic motion, moaned softly. He belonged to Poltorátsky's company, and Poltorátsky, seeing a group of soldiers collected, rode up to them.

"What is it, lad? Been hit?" said Poltorátsky. "Where?"

Avdéev did not answer.

"I was just going to load, your honour, when I heard a click," said a soldier who had been with Avdeev; "and I look and see he's dropped his gun."

"Tut, tut, tut!" Poltorátsky clicked his tongue. "Does it hurt much, Avdéev?"

"It doesn't hurt but it stops me walking. A dropu of vodka now, your honour!"

Some vodka (or rather the spirits drunk by the soldiers in the Caucasus) was found, and Panóv, severely frowning, brought Avdéev a can-lid full. Avdéev tried to drink it, but immediately handed back the lid.

"My soul truns against it," he said. "Drink it yourself."

Panóv drank up the spirit.

Avdéev raised himself but sank back at once. They spread out a cloak and laid him on it.

"Your honour, the colonel is coming," said the sergeant-major to Poltorátsky.

"All right. then will you see to him?" said Poltorátsky and flourishing his whip, he rode at a fast trot to meet Vorontsóv.

Vorontsóv was riding his thoroughbred English chestnut gelding, and was accompanied by the adjutant, a Cossack, and a Chechen interpreter.

"What's happening here?" asked Vorontsóv.

"Why, a skirmishing party attacked our advanced line," Poltorátsky answered.

"Come, come; you've arranged the whole thing yourself!"

"Oh no, Prince, not I," said Poltorátsky with a smile; "they pushed forward of their own accord."

"I hear a soldier has been wounded?"

"Yes, it's a great pity. He's a good soldier."

"Seriously?"

"Seriously, I believe … in the stomach."

"And do you know where I am going?" vorontsov asked.

"I don't."

"Can't you guess?"

"No."

"Hadji Murád has surrendered, and we are now going to meet him."

"You don't mean to say so?"

"His envoy came to me yesterday," said Vorontsóv, with difficulty repressing a smile of joy. "He will be waiting for me at the Shalin glade in a few minutes. Place sharpshooters as far as the glade, and then come and join me." "I understand," said Poltorátsky, lifting his hand to his cap, and rode back to his company. He led the sharpshooters to the right himself, and ordered the seargeant-major to do the same on the left side.

The wounded Avdéev had meanwhile been taken back to the fort by some of the soldiers.

On his way back to rejoin vorontsov, Poltorátsky noticed behind him several horsemen who were overtaking him. In front, on a white-maned horse rode a man of imposing appearance. He wore a turban, and carried weapons with gold ornaments. This man was Hadji Murád. He approached Poltorátsky and said something to him in Tartar. Raising his eye-brows, Poltorátsky made a gesture with his arms to show that he did not understand, and smiled. Hadji Murád gave him smile for smile, and that smile struck Poltorátsky by its childlike kindliness. Poltorátsky had never expected to see the terrible mountain chief look like that. He had expected to see a morose, hard-featured man; and here was a vivacious person whose smile was so kindly that Poltorátsky felt as if he were an old acquaintance. He had but one peculiarity: his eyes, set wide apart, gazed from under their black brows attentively, penetratingly and colmly into the eyes of others.

Hadji Murád's suite consisted of five men. Among them was Khan Mahoma, who had been to see Prince Vorontsóv that night. He was a rosy, round-faced fellow with black lashless eyes and a beaming expression, full of the joy of life. Then there was the Avar Khanefi, a thick-set, hairy man, whose eyebrows joined. He was in charge of all Hadji Murád's property and led a stud-bred horse which carried tightly packed saddle bags. Two men of the suite were particularly striking. The first was a Lesghian: a youth, broad-shouldered but with a waist as slim as a woman's, a brown beard just appearing on his face, and beautiful ram-like eyes. This was Eldár. The other, Gamzálo, was a Chechen, blind in one eye, without eyebrows or eyelashes, with a short red beard, and a scar across his nose and face. Poltorátsky pointed out to Hadji Murdd, Vorontsov, who had just appeared on the road. Hadji MurAd rode to meet him, and, putting his right hand on his heart, said something in Tartar, and stopped. The Chechen interpreter translated.

"He says, 'I surrender myself to the will of the Russian Tsar. I wish to serve him,' he says. 'I wished to so do long ago, but Shamil would not let me.'"

Having heard what the interpreter said, Vorontsóv stretched out his hand in its wash-leather glove to Hadji Murád. Hadji Murád looked at it hestitatingly for a moment, and then pressed it firmly, again saying something, and looking first at the interpreter and then at Vorontsóv.

"He says he did not wish to surrender to any one but you, as you are the son of the Sirdar, and he respects you much."

Vorontsóv nodded to express his thanks. Hadji Murád again said something, pointing to his suite. "He says that these men, his henchmen, will serve the Russians as well as he." Vorontsóv turned towards them and nodded to them too. The merry, black-eyed, lashless Chechen, Khan Mahoma, also nodded, and said something which was probably amusing, for the hairy Avar drew his lips into a smile, showing his ivory-white teeth. But the red-haired Gamzálo's one red eye just glanced at Vorontsóv and then was again fixed on the ears of his horse.

When Vorontsóv and Hadji Murád with their retinues rode back to the fort, the soldiers released from the lines, gathered in groups and made their own comments.

"What a number of souls the damned fellow has destroyed! And now see what a fuss they will make of him!"

"Naturally. He was Shamil's right hand, and now— no fear!"

"Still there's no denying it! he's a fine fellow—a regular *dzhigit!*"[1]

"And the red one? The red on squints at you like a beast!"

"Ugh! He must be a hound!"

They had all specially noticed the red one. Where the wood-felling was going on the soldiers nearest to the road ran out to look. Their officer shouted to them, but Vorontsóv stopped him.

"Let them have a look at their old friend."

"You know who that is?" he added, turning to the nearest soldier, and speaking the words slowly with his English accent.

"No, your Excellency."

"Hadji Murád. ... Heard of him?"

"How could we help it, your Excellency?

We've beaten him many a time!"

"Yes, and we've had it hot from him, too."

"Yes, that's right, your Excellency," answered the soldier, pleased to be talking with his chief.

Hadji Murád understood that they were speaking about him, and smiled brightly with his eyes.

Vornotsóv in the most cheerful mood, returned to the fort.

1. Among the Chechens, a dzhigit is the same as a brave among the Indians, but word is inseparably connected with the idea of skilful hors ernanship.

CHAPTER VI

Young Vorontsóv was much pleased that it was he, and no one else, who had succeeded in winning over and receiving Hadji Murád—next to Shamil Russia's chief and most active enemy. There was just one unpleasant thing about it: General Meller- Zakomelsky was in command of the army at Vozdvizhensky, and the whole affair ought to have been carried out through him; and as Vorontsóv had done everything himself without reporting it, there might be some unpleasantness; and this thought somewhat interfered with his satisfaction. On reaching his house he entrusted Hadji Murád's henchmen to the regimental adjutant and himself showed Hadji Murád into the house.

Princess Mary Vasilevna, elegantly dressed and smiling, and her little son, a handsome curly-headed six year old boy, met Hadji Murád in the drawing-room. The latter placed his hands on his heart, and through the interpreter— who had entered with him —said with solemnity that he regarded himself as the prince's *kunak,* since the prince had brought him into his own house; and that a *kunak's* whole family was as sacred as the *kunak* him self.

Hadji Murád's appearance and manners pleased Mary Vasilevna; and the fact that he flushed when she held out her large white hand to him; inclined her still more in his favour. She invited him to sit down; and having asked him whether he drank coffee, had some served up. He, however, declined it when it came. He understood a little Russian, but could not speak it. When something was said which he could not understand he smiled, and his smile pleased Mary Vasilevna just as it had pleased Poltorátsky. The curly-headed, keen-eyed little boy (whom his mother called Bulka) standing beside her did not take his eyes off Hadji Murád, whom he had always heard spoken of as a great warrior.

Leaving Hadji Murád with his wife, Vorontsóv went to his office to do what was necessary about reporting the fact of Hadji Murád's having come over to the Russians. When he had written a report to the general in command of the left flank—General Kozlovsky—at Grozny, and a letter to his father, Vorontsóv hurried home, afraid that his wife might be vexed with him for forcing on her this terrible stranger, who had to be treated in such a way that he should not take offence, and yet not too kindly. But his fears were needless. Hadji Murád was sitting in an armchair with little Bulka, Vorontsóv's stepson, on his knee; and with bent head was listening attentively to the interpreter, who was translating to him the words of the laughing Marya Vasilevna. Mary

Vasilevna was telling him that if every time a *kunak* admired anything of his he made him a present of it, he would soon have to go about like Adam. …

When the prince entered, Hadji Murád rose at once and, surprising and offending Bulka by putting him off his knee, changed the playful expression of his face to a stern and serious one. He only sat down again when Vorontsóv had himself taken a seat.

Continuing the conversation he answered Marya Vasilevna by telling her that it was a law among his people that anything your *kunak* admired must be presented to him.

"Thy son, kunak!" he said in Russian, patting the curly head of the boy, who had again climbed on his knee.

"He is delightful, your brigand!" said Mary Vasilevna to her husband in French. "Bulka has been admiring his dagger, and he has given it to him."

Bulka showed the dagger to his father.

"C'est un objet de prix!"[1] added she.

"Il faudra trouver l'occasion de lui faire cadeau,"[2] said Vorontsóv.

Hadji Murád, his eyes turned down, sat stroking the boy's curly head and saying: "Dzhigit, dzhigit!"

"A beautiful, beautiful dagger," said Vorontsóv, half drawing out the sharpened blade, which had a ridge down the centre. "I thank thee!"

"Ask him what I can do for him," he said to the interpreter.

The interpreter translated, and Hadji Murád at once replied that he wanted nothing but that he begged to be taken to a place where he could say his prayers.

Vorontsóv called his valet, and told him to do what Hadji Murád desired.

As soon as Hadji Murád was alone in the room allotted to him his face altered. The pleased expression, now kindly and now stately, vanished, and a look of anxiety showed itself. Vorontsóv had received him far better than Hadji Murád had expected. But the better the reception the less did Hadji Murád trust Vorontsóv and his officers. He feared everything: that he might be seized, chained, and sent to Siberia, or simply killed; and therefore he was on his guard. He asked Eldár, when the latter entered his room, where his *murids* had been put, and whether their arms had been taken from them, and where the horses were. Eldár reported that the horses were in the prince's stables; that the men had been placed in a barn; that they retained their arms, and that the interpreter was giving them food and tea.

Hadji Murád shook his head in doubt; and after undressing he said his prayers and told Eldár to bring him his silver dagger. He then dressed, and

1. "It is a thing of value."
2. "We must find an opportunity to make him a present."

having fastened his belt, sat down with his legs on the divan to await what might befall him.

At four in the afternoon the interpreter came to call him to dine with the prince.

At dinner he hardly ate anything except some *pilau*,[3] to which he helped himself from the very part of the dish from which Mary Vasilevna had helped herself.

"He is afraid we shall poison him," Mary Vasilevna remarked to her husband. "He has helped himself from the place where I took my helping." Then, instantly turning to Hadji Murád, she asked him through the interpreter when he would pray again. Hadji Murád lifted five fingers and pointed to the sun. "Then it will soon be time," and Vorontsóv drew out his watch and pressed a spring. The watch struck four and one quarter. This evidently surprised Hadji Murád, and he asked to hear it again, and to be allowed to look at the watch.

"Voila l'occasion! Donnezlui la montre,[4]" said the princess to her husband.

Vorontsóv at once offered the watch to Hadji Murád.

The latter placed his hand on his breast and took the watch. Several times he touched the spring, listened, and nodded his head approvingly.

After dinner, Meller-Zakomelsky's aide-de-camp was announced.

The aide-de-camp informed the prince that the general, having heard of Hadji Murád's arrival, was highly displeased that this had not been reported to him, and required Hadji Murád to be brought to him without delay. Vorontsóv replied that the general's command should be obeyed; and through the interpreter informed Hadji Murád of these orders and asked him to go to Meller with him.

When Mary Vasilevna heard what the aide-de-camp had come about, she at once understood that unpleasantness might arise between her husband and the general, and decided in spite of all her husband's attempts to dissuade her, to go with him and Hadji Murád.

"Vous feriez bien mieux de rester—c'est mon affaire, non pas la votre. …"[5]

"Vous ne pouvez pas m'empecher d'aller voir madame la generale!"

"You could go some other time."

"But I wish to go now!"

There was no help for it, so Vorontsóv agreed; and they all three went.

When they entered, Meller with sombre politeness conducted Mary Vasilevna to his wife and told his aide-de-camp to show Hadji Murád to the waiting room and not to let him out till further orders.

3. An oriental dish prepared with rice and mutton. or chicken.

4. "This is the opportunity !Give him the watch."

5. "You would do much better to remain at home...this is my business, and not yours.

"Please..." he said to Vorontsóv, opening the door of his study and letting the prince enter before him.

Having entered the study he stopped in front of prince and, said without offering him a seat:

"I am in command here and therefore all negotiations with the enemy must be carried on through me! Why did you not report to me that Hadji Murád had come over?"

"An emissary came to me and announced his wish to capitulate only to me," replied Vorontsóv growing pale with excitement, expecting some rude expression from the angry general, and at the same time becoming infected with his anger.

"I ask you why was I not informed?"

"I intended to do so, Baron, but..."

"You are not to address me as 'Baron,' but as 'Your Excellency'!" And here the Baron's pent-up irritation suddenly broke out, and he uttered all that had long been boiling in his soul.

"I have not served my sovereign twenty-seven years in order that men who began their service yesterday, relying on family connections, should give orders under my very nose about matters that do not concern them!"

"Your Excellency, I request you not to say things that are incorrect!" interrupted Vorontsóv.

"I am saying what is correct, and I won't allow..." said the general, still more irritably.

But at that moment Mary Vasilevna entered, rustling with her skirts, and followed by a little modest-looking lady, Meller-Zakomelsky's wife.

"Come, come, Baron! Simon did not wish to displease you," began Marya Vasilevna.

"I am not speaking about that, Princess...."

"Well, you know, let's forget it all that !...You know, 'A bad peace is better than a good quarrel!'...Oh dear, what am I saying?" and she laughed.

The angry general capitulated to the enchanting laugh of the beauty. A smile hovered under his moustache.

"I confess I was wrong," said Vorontsóv, "but—"

"Well, and I too got rather carried away," said Meller, and held out his hand to the prince. Peace was re-established, and it was decided to leave Hadji Murád with the general for the present and then to send him to the commander of the left flank.

Hadji Murád sat in the next room and though he did not understand what was said, he understood what it was necessary for him to understand—namely,

6. "You cannot prevent my going to see the general's wife"!

that they were quarrelling about him, that his desertion of Shamil was a matter of immense importance to the Russians, and that therefore not only would they not exile or kill him, but that he would be able to demand much from them. He also understood that though Meller- Zakomelsky was the commanding-officer, he had not as much influence as his subordinate Vorontsóv; and that Vorontsóv was important and Meller-Zakomelsky unimportant; and therefore when Meller-Zakomelsky sent for him and began to question him, Hadji Murád bore himself proudly and ceremoniously, saying that he had come from the mountains to serve the White Tsar, and would give account only to his Sirdar, meaning the commander-in-chief, Prince Vorontsóv senior, in Tiflis.

CHAPTER VII

The wounded Avdéev was taken to the hospital—a small wooden building roofed with boards, at the entrance of the fort—and was placed on one of the empty beds in the common ward. There were four patients in the ward: one ill with typhus and in high fever; another, pale, with dark shadows under his eyes, who had ague, was just expecting attack and yawned continually; and two more who had been wounded in a raid three weeks before; one in the hand—he was up—and the other in the shoulder. The latter was sitting on a bed. All of them except the typhus patient it peas surrounded and questioned the newcomer, and those who had brought him.

"Sometimes they fire as if peas they were spilling over you, and nothing happens … and this time only aboutfive shots were fired," related one of the bearers.

"Each man get what fate sends!"

"Oh!" groaned Avdéev loudly, trying to master his pain when they began to place him on the bed; but he stopped groaning when he was on it, and only frowned and moved his feet continually. He held his hands over his wound and looked fixedly before him.

The doctor came, and gave orders to turn the wounded man over, to see whether the bullet had passed out behind.

"What's this?" the doctor asked, pointing to the large white scars that crossed one another on the patient's back and loins.

"That was done long ago, your honour!" replied Avdéev, with a groan.

They were the scars left by the flogging Avdéev had received for the money he drank.

Avdéev was again turned over, and the doctor long probed in his stomach for a long time and found the bullet, but failed to extract it. He put a dressing on the wound, and having stuck plaster over it went away. During the whole time the doctor was probing and bandaging the wound Avdéev lay with clenched teeth and closed eyes, but when the doctor had gone he opened them and looked around as though amazed. His eyes were turned on the other patients and on the surgeon's orderly, but he seemed to see not them, but something else that surprised him.

His friends Panóv and Serogin came in; but Avdéev continued to lie in the same position looking before him with surprise. It was long before he recognised his comrades, though his eyes gazed straight at them.

"I say, Peter, have you no message to send home?" said Panóv.

Avdéev did not answer, though he was looking Panóv in the face.

"I say, haven't you any orders to send home?" again repeated Panóv, touching Avdéev's cold, large-boned hand.

Avdéev seemed to come to.

"Ah!...Panóv!"

"Yes, here...I've come! Have you nothing for home? Serogin would write a letter."

"Serogin ..." said Avdéev, moving his eyes with difficulty towards Serogin, "will you write? ... Well then, wrote so: 'Your son,' say 'Peter, has given orders that you should live long[1]. He envied his brother'... I told you about that to-day ...'and now he is himself glad'. Don't worry him...Let him live. God grant it him. I am glad!' Write that."

Having said this he was silent for some time with his eyes fixed on Panóv.

"And did you find your pipe?" he suddenly asked. Panóv did not reply.

"Your pipe...your pipe! I mean, have you found it?" Avdéev repeated.

"It was in my bag."

"That's right!...Well, and now give me a candle to hold...I am going to die,"said Avdéev.

Just then Poltorátsky came in to inquire after his soldier.

"How goes it, my lad! Badly?" said he. Avdéev closed his eyes and shook his head negatively. His broad-cheeked face was pale and stern. He did not reply, but again said to Panóv:

"Bring a candle...I am going to die."

A wax taper was placed in his hand but his fingers would not bend, so it was placed between them and held up for him.

Poltorátsky went away, and five minutes later the orderly put his ear to Avdéev's heart and said that all was over.

Avdéev's death was described in the following manner in the report sent to Tiflis,—

"23rd Nov.—Two companies of the Kurín regiment advanced from the fort on a wood-felling expedition. At midday a considerable number of mountaineers suddenly attacked the wood-fellers. The sharpshooters began to retreat, but the 2nd Company charged with the bayonet and overthrew the mountaineers. In this affair two privates were slightly wounded and one killed. The mountaineers lost about a hundred men killed and wounded.

---

1. A popular expression, meaning that the sender of the message is already dead

CHAPTER VIII

On the day Peter Avdéev died in the hospital at Vozdvizhensk, his old father, with the wife of the brother in whose place he had enlisted, and that brother's daughter—who was already approaching womanhood and almost of age to get married—were threshing oats on the hard-frozen threshing floor.

The day before, there had been a heavy fall of snow followed towards morning by a severe frost. The old man woke when the cocks were crowing for the third time, and seeing the bright moonlight through the frozen window-panes, got down from the oven-top, put on his boots, his sheepskin coat and cap, and went out to the threshing-floor. Having worked there for a couple of hours, he returned to the hut and awoke his son and the women. When the younger woman and the girl came to the threshing-floor they found it ready swept, a wooden shovel sticking in the dry white snow, and beside it birch brooms with the twigs upwards, and two rows of oat-sheaves laid ears to ears in a long line the whole length of the clean threshing-floor. They choose their flails and started threshing, keeping time with their triple blows. The old man struck powerfully with his heavy flail, breaking the straw; the girl struck the ears from above with measured blows; and his daughter-in-law turned the oats over with her flail.

The moon had set, dawn was breaking, and they were finishing the line of sheaves when Akim, the eldest son, in his sheepskin and cap, joined the threshers.

"What are you lazing about for?" shouted his father to him, pausing in his work and leaning on his flail.

"The horses had to be seen to."

"'Horses seen to!'" the father repeated, mimicking him. "The old woman will look after them...Take your flail! You're getting too fat, you drunkard!"

"Have you been standing me treat?" muttered the son.

"What?" said the old man, frowning sternly and missing a stroke.

The son silently took a flail and they began threshing with four flails.

"Trak, tapatam...trak, tapatam...trak..." came down the old man's heavy flail after the three others.

"Why, you've got a nape like a goodly gentleman!...Look here, my trousers have hardly anything to hand on!" said the old man, omitting his stroke and only swinging his flail in the air so as not to get out of time.

They had finished the row, and the women began removing the straw with rakes.

"Peter was a fool to go in your stead. They'd have knocked the nonsense out of you in the army; and he was worth five of such as you at home!"

"That's enough, father," said the daughter-in-law, as she threw aside the binders that had come off the sheaves.

"Yes, feed the six of you, and get no work out of a single one! Peter used to work for two. He was not like..."

Along the trodden path from the house came the old man's wife, the frozen snow creaking under the new bark shoes she wore over her tightly-wound woolen leg-bands. The men were shovelling the unwinnowed grain into heaps, the woman and the girl sweeping up what remained.

"The Elder has been and orders everybody to go and work for the master, carting bricks," said the old woman. "I've got breakfast ready. ... Come along, won't you?"

"All right...Harness the roan and go," said the old man to Akim, "and you'd better look out that you don't get me into trouble as you did the other day!...I can't help regretting Peter!"

"When he was at home you used to scold him," retorted Akim. "Now he's away you keep nagging at me."

"That shows you deserve it,"said his mother in the same angry tones. "You'll never be Peter's equal."

"Well, all right,"said the son.

"'All right,' indeed! You've drunk the meal, and now you say 'all right!'"

"Let bygones be bygones!" said the daughter-in-law.

The disagreements between father and son had begun long ago— almost from the time Peter went as a soldier. Even then the old man felt that he had parted with an eagle for a cuckoo. It is true that it was right—as the old man understood it—for a childless man to go in place of a family man. Akim had four children and Peter had none; but Peter was a worker like his father, skilful, observant, strong, enduring, and above all industrious. He was always at work. If he happened to pass by where people were working he lent a helping hand, as his father would have done, and took a turn or two with the scythe, or loaded a cart, or felled a tree, or chopped some wood. The old man regretted his going away, but there was no help for it. Conscription in those days was like death. A soldier was a severed branch; and to think about him at home was to tear one's heart uselessly. Only occasionally, to prick his elder son, the father mention him, as he had done that day. But his mother often thought of her younger son, and she had long for—more than a year now—she had been asking her husband to send Peter a little money, but the old man had made no reply.

The Kurenkovs were a well-to-do family, and the old man had some savings hidden away; but he would on no account have consented to touch what he had laid by. Now, however his old woman having heard him mention their younger son, made up her mind again to ask him again to send him at least a rouble after selling the oats. This she did. As soon as the young people had gone to work for the proprietor and the old folks were left alone together, she persuaded him to send Peter a rouble out of the oats-money.

So when ninety-six bushels of the winnowed oats had been packed on to three sledges, lined with sacking carefully pinned together at the top with wooden skewers, she gave her old man a letter written at her dictation by the church clerk; and the old man promised when he got to town to enclose a rouble, and to send it off to the right address.

The old man, dressed in a new sheepskin with a homespun cloak over it, his legs wrapped round with warm white woollen leg-bands, took the letter, placed it in his wallet, said a prayer, got into the front sledge, and drove to town. His grandson drove in the last sledge. When he reached town the old man asked the innkeeper to read the letter to him, and listened to it attentively and approvingly.

In her letter Peter's mother first sent him her blessing, then greetings from everybody and the news of his godfather's death; and at the end she added that Aksinya (Peter's wife) had not wished to stay with them but had gone into service, where they heard she was living honestly and well. Then came a reference to that present of a rouble; and finally, in her own words, what the old woman, with tears in her eyes and yielding to her sorrow, had dictated and the church clerk had taken down exactly, word for word:—

"One thing more, my darling child, my sweet dove, my own Peterkin! I have wept my eyes out lamenting for thee, thou light of my eyes. To whom hast thou left me?..."At this point the old woman had sobbed and wept, and said: "That will do!" So the words stood in the letter; but it was not fated that Peter should receive the news of his wife's having left home, nor the present of the rouble, nor his mother's last words. The letter with the money in it came back with the announcement that Peter had been killed in the war, "defending his Tsar, his Fatherland, and the Orthodox Faith." That is how the army clerk expressed it.

The old woman, when this news reached her, wept for as long as she could spare time, and then set to work again. The very next Sunday she went to church and had a requiem chanted, and Peter's name entered among those for whose souls prayers were to be said, and she distributed bits of holy bread to all the good people in memory of Peter, the servant of God.

Aksinya, his widow, also lamented loudly when she heard of her beloved husband death with whom she had lived but one short year. She regretted her husband and her own ruined life; and in her lamentations mentioned Peter's brown locks and his love, and the sadness of her life with her little orphaned

Vanka, and bitterly reproached Peter for having had pity on his brother but none on her—obliged to wander among strangers!

But in the depth of her soul Aksinya was glad of her husband's death. She was pregnant by a shopman with whom she was living; and no one would now have a right to scold her, and the shopman could marry her as he had said he would when he was persuading her to yield he had said he would.

CHAPTER IX

Michael Semenovich Vorontsóv, being the son of the Russian Ambassador, had been educated in England and possessed a European education quite exceptional among the higher Russian officials of his day. He was ambitious, gentle and kind in his manner with inferiors, and a finished courtier with superiors. He did not understand life without power and submission. He had obtained all the highest ranks and decorations and was looked upon as a clever commander, and even as the conquerer of Napoleon at Krasnoye.

In 1852 he was over seventy, but was still quite fresh, moved briskly, and above all was in full possession of a facile refined and agreeable intellect, which he used to maintain his power and to strengthen and spread his popularity. He possessed large means—his own and his wife's (*nee* countess Branitski)—and received an enormous salary as Viceroy, and he spent a great part of his means on building a palace and laying out a garden on the south coast of the Crimea.

On the evening of 4th, December 1852, a courier's *troyka* drew up before his palace in Tiflis. an officer, tired and black with dust, sent by General Kozlovski with the news of Hadji Murád's surrender to the Russians, entered the wide porch, stretching the stiffened muscles of his legs as he passed the sentinel. It was six o'clock, and Vorontsóv was just going in to dinner when he was informed arrival of the courier's. He received him at once, and was therefore a few minutes late for dinner.

When he entered the drawing-room the thirty persons invited to dine, sitting beside Princess Elizabeth Ksaverevna Vorontsóv, or standing in groups by the windows, turned their faces towards him. Vorontsóv was dressed in his usual black military coat, with shoulder-straps but no epaulets, and wore the White Cross of the Order of St. George at his neck.

His clean shaven, foxlike face wore a pleasant smile as, screwing up his eyes, he surveyed the assembly. Entering with quick soft steps he apologised to the ladies for being late, greeted the men, and approaching Princess Manana Orbelyani—a tall, fine, handsome woman of Oriental type about forty-five years of age—he offered her his arm to take her in to dinner. Princess Elizabeth Ksaverevna Vorontsóv gave her arm to a red-haired general with bristly moustaches who was visiting Tiflis. A Georgian prince offered his arm to Princess Vorontsóv's friend, Countess Choiseuil. Doctor Andreevsky, the aide-de-camp, and others, with ladies or without, followed these first couples.

Footmen in livery and knee-breeches drew back and replaced the guests' chairs when they sat down, while the major-domo ceremoniously ladled out steaming soup from a silver tureen.

Vorontsóv took his place in the centre of one side of the long table, and wife sat opposite, with the general on her right. On the prince's right sat his lady, the beautiful Orbelyani; and on his left was a graceful, dark, red-cheeked Georgian woman, glittering with jewels and incessantly smiling.

"Excellentes, chere amie!"[1] replied Vorontsóv to his wife's inquiry about what news the courier had brought him. *"Simon a eu de la chance!"*[2] And he began to tell aloud, so that everyone could hear, the striking news (for him alone not quite unexpected, because negotiations had long been going on) that the bravest and most famous of Shamil's officers, Hadji Murád, had come over to the Russians and would in a day or two be brought to Tiflis.

Everybody—even the young aides-de-camp and officials who sat at the far ends of the table and who had been quietly laughing at something among themselves— became silent and listened.

"And you, General, have you ever met this Hadji Murád?" asked the princess of her neighbour, the carroty general with the bristly mustaches, when the prince had finished speaking.

"More than once, Princess."

And the general went on to tell how Hadji Murád, after the mountaineers had captured Gergebel in 1843, had fallen upon General Pahlen's detachment and killed Colonel Zolotukhin almost before their very eyes.

Vorontsóv listened to the general and smiled amiably, evidently pleased that the latter had joined in the conversation. But suddenly vorontsov's face assumed an absentminded and depressed expression.

The general, having started talking, had begun to tell of his second encounter with Hadji Murád.

"Why, it was he, if your Excellency will please remember," said the General, "who arranged the ambush that attacked the rescue party in the 'Biscuit' expedition."

"Where?" asked Vorontsóv, screwing up his eyes.

What the brave general spoke of as the "rescue" was the affair in the unfortunate Dargo campaign in whicha whole detachment, including Prince Vorontsóv who commanded it, would certainly have perished had it not been rescued by the arrival of fresh troops. Every one knew that the whole Dargo campaign under Vorontsóv's command—in which the Russians lost many killed and wounded and several cannon—had been a shameful affair, and therefore if any one mentioned it in Vorontsóv's presence they did so only in the aspect

1. "Excellent, my dear!"
2. "Simon has had good fortune."

in which Vorontsóv had reported it to the Tsar: as a brilliant achievement of the Russian army. But the word "rescue" plainly indicated that it was not a brilliant victory but a blunder costing many lives. Everybody understood this, and some pretended not to notice the meaning of the general's words, others nervously waited to see what would follow, while a few exchanged glances, and smiled. Only the carroty general with the bristly mustaches noticed nothing, and carried away by his narrative quietly replied,—

"At the rescue, your Excellency."

Having started on his favourite theme, the general recounted circumstantially how Hadji Murád had so cleverly cut the detachment in two that if the rescue party had not arrived (he seemed to be particularly fond of repeating the word "rescue") not a man in the division would have escaped, because…The General did not finish his story, for Manana Orbelyani, having understood what was happening, interrupted him by asking if he had found comfortable quarters in Tiflis. The general, surprised, glanced at everybody all round, and saw his aides-de-camp from the end of the table looking fixedly and significantly at him, and he suddenly understood! Without replying to the princess's question, he frowned, became silent, and began hurriedly swallowing the delicacy that lay on his plate, the appearance and taste of which both completely mystified him.

Everybody felt uncomfortable, but the awkwardness of the situation was relieved by the Georgian prince—a very stupid man but an extraordinarily refined and artful flatterer and courtier—who sat on the other side of Princess Vorontsóva. Without seeming to have noticed anything he began to relate how Hadji Murád had carried off the widow of Akhmet Khan of Mekhtuli.

"He came into the village at night, seized what he wanted, and galloped off again with the whole party."

"Why did he want that particular woman?" asked the princess.

"Oh, he was her husband's enemy, and pursued him but could never once succeed in meeting him right up to the time of his death, so he revenged himself on the widow."

The princess translated this into French to her old friend Countess Choiseuil, who sat next to the Georgian prince.

"Quelle horreur!"[3] said the countess, closing her eyes and shaking her head.

"Oh no!" said Vorontsóv, smiling. "I have been told that he treated his captive with chivalrous respect and afterwards released her."

"Yes, for a ransom!"

"Well, of course. But all the same he acted honourably."

---

3. How horrible

These words of the prince's set the tone for the further conversation. The courtiers understood that the more importance was attributed to Hadji Murád the better pleased the prince would be.

"The man's audacity is amazing. A remarkable man!"

"Why, in 1849, he dashed into Temir Khan Shura and plundered the shops in broad daylight."

An Armenian sitting at the end of the table, who had been in Temir Khan Shura at the time, related the particulars of that exploit of Hadji Murád's.

In fact, Hadji Murád was the sole topic of conversation during the whole dinner.

Everybody in succession praised his courage, his ability, and his magnanimity. Someone mentioned his having ordered twenty six prisoners to be slain; but that too was met by the usual rejoinder, "What's to be done? A la *guerre, comme a la guerre!"*[4]

"He is a great man."

"Had he been born in Europe he might have been another Napoleon," said the stupid Georgian prince with a gift of flattery.

He knew that every mention of Napoleon was pleasant to Vorontsóv, who wore the White Cross at his neck as a reward for having defeated him.

"Well, not Napoleon perhaps, but a gallant cavalry general if you like," said Vorontsóv.

"If not Napoleon, then Murad."

"And his name is Hadji Murád!"

"Hadji Murád has surrendered and now there'll be an end to Shamil also," someone remarked.

"They feel that now" (this "now" meant under Vorontsóv) "they can't hold out," remarked another.

"Tout cela est grace a vous!"[5] said Manana Orbelyani.

Prince Vorontsóv tried to moderate the waves of flattery which began to flow over him. Still, it was pleasant, and in the best of spirits he led his lady back into the drawing room.

After dinner, when coffee was being served in the drawing room, the prince was particularly amiable to everybody, and going up to the general with the red bristly mostaches he tried to appear not to have noticed his blunder.

Having made a round of the visitors, he sat down to the card table. He only played the old-fashioned game of ombre. The prince's partners were the

---

4. "War is war".
5. "And all that, thanks to you!"

Georgian prince, an Armenian general (who had learned the game of ombre from Prince Vorontsóv's valet), and Doctor Andreevsky, a man remarkable for the great influence he exercised.

Placing beside him his gold snuff-box with a portrait of Alexander I on the lid, the prince tore open a pack of highly glazed cards and was going to spread them out when his Italian valet brought him a letter on a silver tray.

"Another courier, your Excellency."

Vorontsóv laid down the cards, excused himself, opened the letter, and began to read.

The letter was from his son, who described Hadji Murád's surrender and his own encounter with Meller- Zakomelsky.

The princess came up and inquired what their son had written.

"It's all about the same matter… *Il a eu quelques desagrements avec le commandant de la place. Simon a eu tort*[6]…But 'All's well that ends well,'" he added in English, handing the letter to his wife; and turning to his respectfully waiting partners he asked them to draw cards.

When the first round had been dealt Vorontsóv did what he was in the habit of doing when in a particularly pleasant mood: with his white, wrinkled old hand he took out a pinch of French snuff, carried it to his nose, and released it.

6. "He has had unpleasantness with the commander of the place. Simon in the wrong."

CHAPTER X

When next day, Hadji Murád appeared at the prince's palace the waiting room was already full of people. Yesterday's general with the bristly moustaches was there in full uniform with all his decorations, having come to take leave. There was the commander of a regiment who was in danger of being court martialled for misappropriating commisarriat money, and there was a rich Armenian (patronised by Doctor Andreevsky) who wanted to get from the Government a renewal of his monopoly for the sale of vodka. There, dressed in black, was the widow of an officer who had been killed in action. She had come to ask for a pension, or for free education for her children. There was a ruined Georgian prince in a magnificent Georgian costume who was trying to obtain for himself some confiscated Church property. There was an official with a large roll of paper containing a new plan for subjugating the Caucasus. There was also a Khan who had come solely to be able to tell his people at home that he had called on the prince. They all waited their turn and were one by one shown into the prince's cabinet and out again by the aide-de-camp, a handsome, fair-haired youth.

When Hadji Murád entered the waiting room with his brisk though limping step all eyes were turned towards him and he heard his name whispered from various parts of the room.

He was dressed in a long white Circassian coat over a brown *beshmet* trimmed round the collar with fine silver lace. He wore black leggings and soft shoes of the same colour which were stretched over his instep as tight as gloves. On his head he wore a high cap, draped turban- fashion—that same turban for which, on the denunciation of Akhmet Khan, he had been arrested by General Klugenau, and which had been the cause of his going over to Shamil.

Hadji Murád stepped briskly across the parquet floor of the waiting-room, his whole slender figure swaying slightly in consequence of his lameness in one leg, which was shorter than the other. His eyes, set far apart, looked calmly before him and seemed to see no one.

The handsome aide-de-camp, having greeted him, asked him to take a seat while he went to announce him to the prince, but Hadji Murád declined to sit down, and, putting his hand on his dagger, stood with one foot advanced, looking round contemptuously at all those present.

The prince's interpreter, Prince Tarkhanov, approached Hadji Murád and spoke to him. Hadji Murád answered abruptly and unwillingly. A Kumyk prince, who was there to lodge a complaint against a police official, came out of the prince's room, and then the aide-de-camp called Hadji Murád, led him to the door of the cabinet, and showed him in.

Vorontsov received Hadji Murád standing beside his table. The old white face of the Commander-in-Chief did not wear yesterday's smile but was rather stern and solemn.

On entering the large room with its enormous table and great windows ith green venetian blinds, Hadji Murád placed his small sunburnt hands on his chest just where the front of his white coat overlapped, and lowering his eyes began, without hurrying, to speak distinctly and respectfully, using the Kumyk dialect, which he spoke well.

"I place myself under the powerful protection of the great Tsar and of yourself," said he, "and promise to serve the White Tsar in faith and truth to the last drop of my blood, and I hope to be useful to you in the war with Shamil who is my enemy and yours."

Having heard the interpreter out, Vorontsóv glanced at Hadji Murád and Hadji Murád glanced at Vorontsóv.

The eyes of the two men met, and expressed to each other much that could not have been put into words, and that was not at all what the interpreter said. Without words they told each other the whole truth. Vorontsóv's eyes said that he did not believe a single word Hadji Murád was saying, and that he knew he was and always would be an enemy to everything Russian and had surrendered only because he was obliged to. Hadji Murád understood this and yet continued to give assurances of his fidelity. His eyes said, "That old man ought to be thinking of his death, and not of war, old but though he is he is cunning, and I must be careful." Vorontsóv understood this also, but nevertheless spoke to Hadji Murád in the way he considered necessary for the success of the war.

"Tell him," said Vorontsóv, "that our sovereign is as merciful as he is mighty and will probably at my request pardon him and take him into his service… Have you told him?" he asked looking at Hadji Murád?…"Until I receive my master's gracious decision, tell him I take it on myself to receive him and make his sojourn among us pleasant."

Hadji Murád again pressed his hands to the centre of his chest and began to say something with animation.

"He says," the interpreter translated, "that formerly, when he governed Avaria in 1839, he served the Russians faithfully and would never have deserted them had not his enemy, Akhmet Khan, wishing to ruin him, calumniated him to General Klugenau."

"I know, I know," said Vorontsóv (though if he had ever known he had long forgotten it). "I know," said he sitting down and motioning Hadji Murád to the divan that stood beside the wall. But Hadji Murád did not sit down.

Shrugging his powerful shoulders as a sign that he could not bring himself to sit in the presence of so important a man, he went on, addressing the interpreter,—

"Akhmet Khan and Shamil are both my enemies. Tell the prince that Akhmet Khan is dead and I cannot revenge myself on him, but Shamil lives and I will not die without taking vengeance on him," said he, knitting his brows and tightly closing his mouth.

"Yes, yes; but how does he want to revenge himself on Shamil?" said Vorontsóv quietly to the interpreter. "And tell him he may sit down."

Hadji Murád again declined to sit down, and in answer to the question replied that his object in coming over to the Russians was to help them to destroy Shamil.

"Very well, very well," said Vorontsóv; "but what exactly does he wish to do? … Sit down, sit down."

"Hadji Murad again declined to sit down, and in answer to the question replied that his object in coming over to the Russians was to help them to destroy Shamil

"Very well, very well," said Vorontsov; "but what exactly does he wish to do? … Sit down, sit down!"

Hadji Murád sat down, and said that if only they would send him to the Lesghian line and would give him an army, he would guarantee to raise the whole of Daghestan, and Shamil would then be unable to hold out.

"That would be excellent. … I'll think it over," said Vorontsóv.

The interpreter translated Vorontsóv's words to Hadji Murád.

Hadji Murád pondered.

"Tell the Sirdar one thing more," Hadji Murád began again, "that my family are in the hands of my enemy, and that as long as they are in the mountains I am bound and cannot serve him. Shamil would kill my wife and my mother and my children if I went openly against him. Let the prince first exchange my family for the prisoners he has, and then I will destroy Shamil or die!"

"All right, all right," said Vorontsóv. "I will think it over. … Now let him go to the chief of the staff and explain to him in detail his position, intentions, and wishes."

Thus ended the first interview between Hadji Murád and Vorontsóv.

That evening at the new theater, which was decorated in Oriental style. Italian opera was performed.Vorontsóv was in his box when the striking figure of the limping Hadji Murád wearing a turban appeared in the stalls. He came in with Loris-Melikov,[1] Vorontsóv's aide-de-camp, in whose charge he was

1. Count Michael Tarielovitch Loris- Melikov, who after- wards became Minister of the Interior, and framed the Liberal ukase which was signed by Alexander II. the day that he was assassinated

placed, and took a seat in the front row. Having sat through the first act with Oriental Mohammedan dignity, expressing no pleasure but, only obvious indifference, he rose and looking calmly round at the audience went out, drawing to himself everybody's attention.

The next day was Monday and there was the usual evening party at the Vorontsóvs'. In the large brightly lighted hall a band was playing, hidden among trees. Young not very young and women wearing dresses that displayed their bare necks, arms, and breasts, turned round and round in the embrace of men in bright uniforms. At the buffet, footmen in red swallow- tail coats and wearing shoes and knee-breeches, poured out champagne and served sweetmeats to the ladies. The "Sirdar's" wife also, in spite of her age, went about half-dressed among the visitors affably, smiling and through the interpreter said a few amiable words to Hadji Murád who glanced at the visitors with the same indifference he had shown yesterday in the theater. After the hostess, other half-naked women came up to him, and all of them stood shamelessly before him and smilingly asked him the same question: How he liked what he saw? Vorontsóv himself, wearing gold epaulet and gold shoulder-knots with his white cross and ribbon at his neck, came up and asked him the same question, evidently feeling sure, like all the others, that Hadji Murád could not help being pleased at what he saw. Hadji Murád replied to Vorontsóv as he had replied to them all, that among his people nothing of the kind was done, without expressing an opinion as to whether it was good or bad that it was so.

Here at the ball Hadji Murád tried to speak to Vorontsóv about buying out his family; but Vorontsóv, pretending he had not heard him, walked away, and Loris-Melikov afterwards told Hadji Murád that this was the place to talk about business.

When it struck eleven Hadji Murád, having made sure of the time by the watch the Vorontsóvs had given him, asked Loris-Melikov whether he might now leave. Loris- Melikov said he might, though it would be better to stay. In spite of this Hadji Murád did not stay, but drove in the phaeton placed at his disposal to the quarters that had been assigned to him.

CHAPTER XI

On the fifth day of Hadji Murád's stay in Tiflis, Loris-Melikov, the Viceroy's aide-de-camp, came to see him at the latter's command.

"My head and my hands are glad to serve the Sirdar," said Hadji Murád with his usual diplomatic expression, bowing his head and putting his hands to his chest. "Command me!" said he, looking amiably into Loris-Melikov's face.

Loris-Melikov sat down in an arm chair placed by the table and Hadji Murád sank on to a low divan opposite and, resting his hands on his knees, bowed his head and listened attentively to what the other said to him.

Loris-Melikov, who spoke Tartar fluently, told him that though the prince knew about his past life, he yet wanted to hear the whole story from himself.

"Tell it me, and I will write it down and translate it into Russian and the prince will send it to the Emperor."

Hadji Murád remained silent for a while (he never interrupted anyone, but always waited to see whether his collocutor had not something more to say), then he raised his head, shook back his cap, and smiled the peculiar childlike smile that had captivated Mary Vasilevna.

"I can do that," said he, evidently flattered by the thought that his story would be read by the Emperor.

"Thou must tell me" (nobody is addressed as "you") "everything, deliberately from the beginning," said Loris Melikov drawing a notebook from his pocket.

"I can do that, only there is much—very much—to tell! Many events have happened!" said Hadji Murád.

"If thou canst not do it all in one day thou wilt finish it another time," said Loris-Melikov.

"Shall I begin at the beginning?"

"Yes, at the very beginning...where thou wast born and where thou didst live."

Hadji Murád's head sank and he sat in that position for a long time. Then he took a stick that lay beside the divan, drew a little knife with an ivory gold-inlaid handle, sharp as a razor, from under his dagger, and started whittling the stick with it and speaking at the same time.

"Write: Born in Tselmess, a small *aoul,* 'the size of an ass's head,' as we in the mountains say," he began. "not far from it, about two cannon-shots, lies Khunzakh where the Khans lived. Our family was closely connected with them.

"My mother, when my eldest brother Osman was born, nursed the eldest Khan, Abu Nutsal Khan. Then she nursed the second son of the Khan, Umma Khan, and reared him; but Akhmet my second brother died, and when I was born and the Khansha[1] bore Bulach Khan, my mother would not go as wet-nurse again. My father ordered her to, but she would not. She said: 'I should again kill my own son and I will not go.' Then my father, who was passionate, struck her with a dagger and would have killed her had they not rescued her from him. So she did not give me up, and later on she composed a song...but I need not tell that."

"Well, so my mother did not go as nurse," he said with a jerk of his head, "and the Khansha took another nurse but still remained fond of my mother; and my mother used to take us children to the Khansha's palace, and we played with her children and she was fond of us.

"There were three young Khans: Abu Nutsal Khan my brother Osman's foster-brother; Umma Khan my own sworn brother; and Bulach Khan the youngest—whom Shamil threw over the precipice. But that happened later.

"I was about sixteen when *murids* began to visit the *aouls.* They beat the stones with wooden scimitars and cried 'Mussulmans, *Ghazavat!'* The Chechens all went over to Muridism and the Avars began to go over too. I was then living in the palace like a brother of the Khans. I could do as I liked, and I became rich. I had horses and weapons and money. I lived for pleasure and had no care, and went on like that till the time when Kazi-Mulla, the Imam, was killed and Hamzad succeeded him. Hamzad sent envoys to the Khans to say that if they did not join the *Ghazavat* he would destroy Khunzakh.

"This needed consideration. The Khans feared the Russians, but were also afraid to join in the Holy War. The old Khansha sent me with her second son, Umma Khan, to Tiflis to ask the Russian Commander-in-Chief for help against Hamzad. The Commander-in-Chief at Tiflis was Baron Rosen. He did not receive either me or Umma Khan. He sent word that he would help us, but did nothing. Only his officers came riding to us and played cards with Umma Khan. They made him drunk with wine and took him to bad places, and he lost all he had to them at cards. His body was as strong as a bull's and he was as brave as a lion, but his soul was weak as water. He would have gambled away his last horses and weapons if I had not made him come away.

"After visiting Tiflis my ideas changed and I advised the old Khansha and the Khans to join the *Ghazavat...*"

1. Khansha, Khan's wife

"What made you change your mind?" asked Loris- Melikov. "Were you not pleased with the Russians?"

Hadji Murád paused.

"No, I was not pleased," he answered decidedly, closing his eyes."and there was also another reason why I wished to join the *Ghazavat."*

"What was that?"

"Why, near Tselmess the Khan and I encountered three murids, two of whom escaped but the third one I shot with my pistol.

"He was still alive when I approached to take his weapons. He looked up at me, and said, 'Thou has killed me…I am happy; but thou are a Mussulman, young and strong. Join the *Ghazavat!* God wills it!'"

"And did you join it?"

"I did not, but it made me think," said Hadji Murád, and he went on with his tale.

"When Hamzad approached Kunzakh we sent our Elders to him to say that we would agree to join the *Ghazavat* if the Imam would sent a learned man to us to explain it to us.

Hamzad had our Elders' moustaches shaved off, their nostrils pierced, and cakes hung to their noses, and in that condition he sent them back to us.

"The Elders brought word that Hamzad was ready to send a sheik to teach us the *Ghazavat,* but only if the Khansha sent him her youngest son as a hostage. She took him at his word, and sent her youngest son, Bulach Khan. Hamzad received him well, and sent to invite the two elder brothers also. He sent word that he wished to serve the Khans as his father had served their father…The Khansha was a weak, stupid, and conceited woman, as all women are when they are not under control. She was afraid to send away both sons and sent only Umma Khan. I went with him. We were met by *murids* about a mile before we arrived and they sang and shot and caracoled around us; and when we drew near, Hamzad came out of his tent and went up to Umma Khan's stirrup and received him as a Khan. He said,—

'I have not done any harm to thy family and do not wish to do any. Only do not kill me and do not prevent my bringing the people over to the *Ghazavat,* and I will serve you with my whole army, as my father served your father! Let me live in your house and I will help you with my advice, and you shall do as you like!'

"Umma Khan was slow of speech. He did not know how to reply and remained silent. Then I said that if this was so, let Hamzad come to Khunzakh and the Khansha and the Khans would receive him with honour…but I was not allowed to finish—and here I first encountered Shamil, who was beside the Imam. He said to me.

"Thou has not been asked. … It was the Khan!"

"I was silent, and Hamzad led Umma Khan into his tent. Afterwards Hamzad called me and ordered me to go to Kunzakh with his envoys. I went. The envoys began persuading the Khansha to send her eldest son also to Hamzad. I saw there was treachery, and told her not to send him; but a woman has as much sense in her head as an egg has hair. She ordered her son to go. Abu Nutsal Khan did not wish to. Then she said, 'I see thou are afraid!' Like a bee she knew where to sting him most painfully. Abu Nutsal Khan flushed, and did not speak to her any more, but ordered his horse to be saddled. I went with him.

"Hamzad met us with even greater honour than he had shown Umma Khan. He himself rode out two rifle-shot lengths down the hill to meet us. A large party of horsemen with their banners followed him, and they too sang, shot, and caracoled.

"When we reached the camp, Hamzad led the Khan into his tent, and I remained with the horses…

"I was some way down the hill when I heard shots fired in Hamzad's tent. I ran there and saw Umma Khan lying prone in a pool of blood, and Abu Nutsal was fighting the *murids.* One of his cheeks had been hacked off, and hung down. He supported it with one hand, and with the other stabbed with his dagger at all who came near him. I saw him strike down Hamzad's brother and aim a blow at another man; but then the *murids* fired at him and he fell."

Hadji Murád stopped and his sunburnt face flushed a dark red and his eyes became bloodshot.

"I was seized with fear and ran away."

"Really?… I thought thou never wast afraid," said Loris-Melikov. "Never after that…Since then I have always remembered that shame, and when I recalled it I feared nothing!"

CHAPTER XII

But enough! It is time for me to pray," said Hadji Murád drawing from an inner breast-pocket of his Circassian coat Vorontsóv's repeater watch and carefully pressing the spring. The repeater struck twelve and a quarter. Hadji Murád listened with his head on one side, repressing a childlike smile.

"Kunak Vorontsóv's present," he said, smiling.

"It is a good watch," said Loris-Melikov. "Well then, go thou and pray, and I will wait." "*Yakshi.* Very well," said Hadji Murád and went to his bedroom.

Left by himself, Loris-Melikov wrote down in his notebook the chief things Hadji Murád had related; and then lighting a cigarette, began to pace up and down the room. On reaching the door opposite the bedroom he heard animated voices speaking rapidly in Tartar. He guessed that the speakers were Hadji Murád's *murids*, and opening the door he went to them.

The room was impregnated with that special leathery acid smell peculiar to the mountaineers. On a *búrka* spread out on the floor sat the one-eyed, red-haired Gamzálo, in a tattered greasy *beshmet,* plaiting a bridle. He was saying something excitedly, speaking in a hoarse voice, but when Loris-Melikov entered he immediately became silent and continued his work without paying any attention to him.

In front of Gamzálo stood the merry Khan Mahoma, showing his white teeth, his black lashless eyes glittering, and saying something over and over again. The handsome Eldár, his sleeves turned up on his strong arms, was polishing the girths of a saddle suspended from a nail. Khanefi, the principal worker and manager of the household, was not there he was cooking their dinner in the kitchen.

"What were you disputing about?" asked Loris- Melikov after greeting them.

"Why, he keeps on praising Shamil," said Khan Mahoma giving his hand to Loris-Melikov. "He says Shamil is a great man, learned, holy, and a *dzhigit."*

"How is it that he has left him and still praises him?"

"He has left him and still praises him," repeated Khan Mahoma, his teeth showing and his eyes glittering.

"And does he really consider him a saint?" asked Loris-Melikov.

"If he were not a saint the people would not listen to him," said Gamzálo rapidly.

"Shamil is no saint, but Mansur was!" replied Khan Mahoma. "He was a real saint. When he was Imam the people were quite different. He used to ride through the *aouls,* and the people used to come out and kiss the hem of his coat and confess their sins and vow to do no evil. Then all the people—so the old men say—lived like saints: not drinking, nor smoking, nor neglecting their prayers, and forgiving one another their sins even when blood had been spilt. If anyone then found money or anything, he tied it to a stake and set it up by the roadside. In those days God gave the people success in everything—not as now."

"In the mountains they don's smoke or drink now," said Gamzálo.

"Your Shamil is a l*amorey,* "said Khan Mahoma, winking at Loris-Melikov. (*Lamorey* was a contemptuous term for a mountaineer.)

"Yes, *lamorey* means mountaineer," replied Gamzálo."It is in the mountains that the eagles dwell."

"Smart fellow! Well hit!" said Khan Mahoma with a grin, pleased at his adversary's apt retort.

Seeing the silver cigarette-case in Loris Melikov's hand, Khan Mahoma asked for a cigarette, and when Loris-Melikov remarked that they were forbidden to smoke, he winked with one eye and jerking his head in the direction of Hadji Murád's bedroom replied that they could do it as long as they were not seen. He at once began smoking—not inhaling—and pouting his red lips awkwardly as he blew out the smoke.

"That is wrong!" said Gamzálo severely, and left the room for a time .

Khan Mahoma winked after him, and while smoking asked Loris-Melikov where he could best buy a silk *beshmet* and a white cap.

"Why, has thou so much money?"

"I have enough," replied Khan Mahoma with a wink.

"Ask him where he got the money," said Eldár, turning his handsome smiling face towards Loris-Melikov.

"Oh, I won it!" said Khan Mahoma quickly, and related how while walking in Tiflis the day before, he had come upon a group of men—Russians and Armenians—playing at *orlyanka* (a kind of heads-and-tails). the stake was a large one: three gold; pieces and much silver. Khan Mahoma at once saw what the game consisted in, and jingling the coppers he had in his pocket he went up to the players and said he would stake the whole amount.

"How couldst thou do it? Hadst thou so much?" asked Loris-Melikov.

"I had only twelve kopecks," said Khan Mahoma, grinning.

"Well but if thou hadst lost?"

"Why, look here!"said Khan Mahoma, pointing to his pistol.

"Wouldst thou have given that?"

"Why give it? I should have run away, and if any one had tried to stop me I should have killed him—that's all!"

"Well, and didst thou win?"

"Aye, I won it all and went away!"

Loris-Melikov quite understood what sort of men Khan Mahoma and Eldár were. Khan Mahoma was a merry fellow, careless and ready for any spree. He did not know what to do with his superfluous vitality. He was always gay and reckless, and played with his own and other people's lives. For the sake of that sport with life he had now come over to the Russians, and for the same sport he might go back to Shamil to-morrow.

Eldár was also quite easy to understand. He was a man entirely devoted to his *murshid;* calm, strong, and firm.

The red-haired Gamzálo was the only one Loris-Melikov did not understand. He saw that that man was not only loyal to Shamil, but felt an insuperable aversion, contempt, repugnance, and hatred for all Russians; and Loris-Melikov could therefore not understand why he had come over to them. It occurred to him that, as some of the higher officials suspected, Hadji Murád's surrender, and his tales of hatred of Shamil might be false, and that perhaps he had surrendered only to spy out the Russians' weak spots, that-after escaping back to the mountains-he might be able to direct his forces accordingly. Gamzálo's whole person strengthened this suspicion.

"The others, and Hadji Murád himself, know how to hid their intentions, but this one betrays them by his open hatred," thought he.

Loris-Melikov tried to speak to him. He asked whether he did not feel dull. "No, I don't!" he growled hoarsely without stopping his work, and glancing at his questioner out of the corner of his one eye. He replied to all Loris-Melikov's other questions in a similar manner.

While Loris-Melikov was in the room, Hadji Murád's fourth *murid* came in, the Avar Khanefi; a man with a hairy face and neck and an arched chest as rough as if it were overgrown with moss. He was strong, and a hard worker, always engrossed in his duties, and like Eldár unquestioningly obedient to his master.

When he entered the room to fetch some rice, Loris-Melikov stopped him and asked where he came from and how long he had been with Hadji Murád.

"Five years," replied Khanefi. "I come from the same *aoul* as he. My father killed his uncle and they wished to kill me." he said calmly, looking from under his joined eye-brows straight into Loris-Melikov's face.

"Then I asked them to adopt me as a brother.""What do you mean by 'adopt as a brother'?"

"I did not shave my head nor cut my nails for two months, and then I came to them. They let me in to Patimat, his mother, and she gave me the breast and I became his brother."

Hadji Murád's voice could be heard from the next room, and Eldár, immediately answering his call, promptly wiped his hands and went with large strides into the drawing-room.

"He asks thee to come," said he, coming back.

Loris-Melikov gave another cigarette to the merry Khan Mahoma and went into the drawing, room.

CHAPTER XIII

When Loris-Melikov entered the drawing-room Hadji Murád received him with a bright face.

"Well, shall I continue?"he asked, sitting down comfortably on the divan.

"Yes, certainly,"said Loris-Melikov."I have been in to have a talk with thy henchmen...One is a jolly fellow!"he added.

"Yes, Khan Mahoma is a frivolous fellow,"said Hadji Murád.

"I liked the young handsome one."

"Ah, that's Eldár. He's young but firm—made of iron!"

They were silent for a while.

"So I am to go on?"

"Yes, yes!"

"I told the how the Khans were killed...Well, having killed them, Hamzad rode into Khunzakh and took up his quarters in their palace. The Khansha was the only one of the family left alive. Hamzad sent for her. She reproached him, so he winked to his *murid,* Aseldar, who struck her from behind and killed her."

"Why did he kill her?" asked Loris-Melikov.

"What could he do?...Where the fore legs have gone, the hind legs must follow! He killed off the whole family. Shamil killed the youngest son—threw him over a precipice...

"Then the whole of Avaria surrendered to Hamzad. But my brother and I would not surrender. We wanted his blood for the blood of the Khans. We pretended to yield, but our only thought was how to get his blood. We consulted our grandfather, and decided to await the time when he would come out of his palace, and then to kill him from an ambush. Someone overheard us and told Hamzad, who sent for grandfather, and said, 'Mind, if it be true that thy grandsons are planning evil against me, thou and they shall hang from one rafter. I do God's work, and cannot be hindered...Go, and remember what I have said!'

"Our grandfather came home and told us.

"Then we decided not to wait, but to do the deed on the first day of the feast in the mosque. Our comrades would not take part in it, but my brother and I remained firm.

"We took two pistols each, put on our *búrka*s, and went to the mosque. Hamzad entered the mosque with thirty *murids*. They all had drawn swords in their hands. Aseldar, his favourite *murid* (the one who had cut off Khansha), saw us, shouted to us to take off our *búrka*s, and came towards me. I had my dagger in my hand and I killed him with it and rushed at Hamzad; but my brother Osman had already shot him. He was still alive and rushed at my brother dagger in hand, but I have him a finishing blow on the head. There were thirty *murids* and we were only two. They killed my brother Osman, but I kept them at bay, leapt through the window, and escaped.

"When it was known that Hamzad had been killed, all the people rose. The *murids* fled, and those of them who did not flee were killed."

Hadji Murád paused, and breathed heavily.

"That was very well," he continued, "but afterwards everything was spoilt.

"Shamil succeeded Hamzad. He sent envoys to me to say that I should join him in attacking the Russians, and that if I refused he would destroy Khunzakh and kill me.

"I answered that I would not join him, and would not let him come to me..."

"Why didst thou not go with him?"asked Loris-Melikov.

Hadji Murád frowned and did not reply at once.

"I could not. The blood of my brother Osman and of Abu Nutsal Khan was on his hands. I did not go to him. General Rosen sent me an officer's commission and ordered me to govern Avaria. All this would have been well, but that Rosen appointed as Khan of Kazi- Kumukh, first Mahomet-Murza, and afterwards Akhmet Khan, who hated me. He had been trying to get the Khansha's daughter, Sultanetta, in marriage for his son, but she would not giver her to him, and he believed me to be the cause of this... Yes, Akhmet an hated me and sent his henchmen to kill me, but I escaped from them. Then he spoke ill of me to General Klugenau. He said that I told the Avars not to supply wood to the Russian soldiers, and he also said that I had donned a turban—this one" Hadji Murád touched his turban "and that this meant that I had gone over to Shamil. The General did not believe him, and gave orders that I should not be touched. But when the General went to Tiflis, Akhmet Khan did as he pleased. He sent a company of soldiers to seize me, put me in chains, and tied me to a cannon.

"So they kept me six days," he continued. "On the seventh day they untied me and started to take me to Temir-Khan-Shura. Forty soldiers with loaded guns had me in charge. My hands were tied and I knew that they had orders to kill me if I tried to escape.

"As we approached Mansokha the path became narrow, and on the right was an abyss about a hundred and twenty yards deep. I went to the right—to the very edge. A soldier wanted to stop me, but I jumped down and pulled him with me. He was killed outright, but I, as you see, remained alive.

"Ribs, head, arms, and leg—all were broken! I tried to crawl, but grew giddy and fell asleep. I awoke, wet with blood. A shepherd saw me, and called some people who carried me to an *aoul*. My ribs and head healed, and my leg too, only it has remained short," and Hadji Murád stretched out his crooked leg. "It still serves me, however, and that is well," said he.

"The people heard the news, and began coming to me. I recovered, and went to Tselmess. The Avars again called on me to rule over them," said Hadji Murád, with tranquil, confident pride, "and I agreed."

He quickly rose, and taking a portfolio out of a saddle-bag, drew out two discoloured letters and handed one of them to Loris-Melikov. They were from General Klugenau. Loris-Melikov read the first letter, which was as follows.—

"Lieutenant Hadji Murád, thou has served under me, and I was satisfied with thee, and considered thee a good man.

"Recently Akhmet Khan informed me that thou are a traitor, that thou has donned a turban, and has intercourse with Shamil, and that thou has taught the people to disobey the Russian Government. I ordered thee to be arrested and brought before me but thou fledst. I do not know whether this is for thy good or not, as I do not know whether thou art guilty or not.

"Now hear me. If thy conscience is pure, if thou are not guilty in anything towards the great Tsar, come to me, fear no one. I am thy defender. The Khan can do nothing to thee, he is himself under my command, so thou has nothing to fear."

Klugenau added that he always kept his word and was just, and he again exhorted Hadji Murád to appear before him.

When Loris-Melikov had read this letter, Hadji Murád, before handing him the second one, told him what he had written in reply to the first.

"I wrote that I wore a turban, not for Shamil's sake, but for my soul's salvation; that I neither wished nor could go over to Shamil, because he had cause the death of my father's, my brothers, and my relations; but that I could not join the Russians because I had been dishonoured by them. (In Khunzakh, while I was bound, a scoundrel had spat on me and I could not join your people until that man was killed.) But, above all, I feared that liar, Akhmet Khan.

"Then the General sent me this letter," said Hadji Murád, handing Loris-Melikov the other discolored paper.

"Thou has answered my first letter and I thank thee," read Loris-Melikov. "Thou writest that thou are not afraid to return, but that the insult done thee by a certain Giaour prevents it, but I assure thee that the Russian law is just, and that thou shalt see him who dared to offend thee punished before thine eyes. I have already given orders to investigate the matter.

"Hear me, Hadji Murád! I have a right to be displeased with thee for not trusting me and my honour, but I forgive thee, for I know how suspicious mountaineers are in general. If thy conscience is pure, if thou hast put on a turban only for they soul's salvation, then thou art right, and mayst look me and the Russian Government boldly in the eye. He who dishonoured thee shall, I assure thee, be punished; and *thy property shall be restored to thee,* and thou shalt see and know what Russian law is. And besides, we Russians look at things differently, and thou has not sunk in our eyes because some scoundrel has dishonoured thee.

"I myself have consented to the Chimrints wearing turbans, and I regard their actions in the right light, and therefore I repeat that thou hast nothing to fear. Come to me with the man by whom I am sending thee this letter. He is faithful to me and is not the slave of thy enemies but is the friend of a man who enjoys the special favour of the Government.

" Further on Klugenau again tried to persuade Hadji Murád to come over to him.

"I did not believe him," said Hadji Murád when Loris-Melikov had finished reading, "and did not go to Klugenau. The chief thing for me was to revenge myself on Akhmet Khan, and that I could not do through the Russians. Then Akhmet Khan surrounded Tselmess and wanted to take me or kill me. I had too few men and could not drive him off, and just then came an envoy with a letter from Shamil, promising to help me to defeat and kill Akhmet Khan, and making me ruler over the whole of Avaria. I considered the matter for a long time and then went over to Shamil, and from that time I have fought the Russians continually."

Here Hadji Murád related all his military exploits, of which there were very many, and some of which were already familiar to Loris-Melikov. All his campaigns and raids had been remarkable for the extraordinary rapidity of his movements and the boldness of his attacks, which were always crowned with success.

"There never was any friendship between me and Shamil," said Hadji Murád at the end of his story, "but he feared me and needed me. But it so happened that I was asked who should be Imam after Shamil, and I replied: 'He will be Imam whose sword is sharpest!'

"This was told to Shamil, and he wanted to get rid of me. He sent me into Tabasaran. I went, and captured a thousand sheep and three hundred horses, but he said I had not done the right thing, and dismissed me from being Naib, and ordered me to send him all the money. I sent him a thousand gold pieces. He sent his *murids* and they took from me all my property. He demanded that I should go to him, but I knew he wanted to kill me and I did not go. Then he sent to take me. I resisted, and went over to Vorontsóv. Only I did not take my family. My mother, my wives, and my son are in his hands. Tell the Sirdar that as long as my family is in Shamil's power I can do nothing."

"I will tell him," said Loris-Melikov.

"Take pains, try hard!...What is mine is thine, only help me with the Prince. I am tied up and the end of the rope is in Shamil's hands," said Hadji Murád concluding his story.

CHAPTER XIV

On the 20th of December Vorontsóv wrote as follows to Chernyshov, the Minister of War. The letter was in French:

"I did not write to you by the last post, dear Prince, as I wished first to decide what we should do with Hadji Murád, and for the last two or three days I have not been feeling quite well.

"In my last letter I informed you of Hadji Murád's arrival here. He reached Tiflis on the 8th, and next day I made his acquaintance; and during the following seven or eight days have spoken to him and considered what use we can make of him in the future, and especially what we are to do with him at present; for he is much concerned about the fate of his family, and with every appearance of perfect frankness says that while they are in Shamil's hands he is paralysed and cannot render us any service, or show his gratitude for the friendly reception and forgiveness we have extended to him.

"His uncertainty about those dear to him makes him fervish, and the persons I have appointed to live with him assure me that he does not sleep at night, eats hardly anything, prays continually, and asks only to be allowed to ride out accompanied by several Cossacks—the sole recreation and exercise possible for him and made necessary to him by lifelong habit. Every day he comes to me to know whether I have any news of his family, and to ask me to have all the prisoners in our hands collected and offered to Shamil in exchange for them. He would also give a little money. There are people who would let him have some for the purpose. He keeps repeating to me: 'Save my family and then give me a chance to serve you' (preferably, in his opinion, on the Lesghian line), 'and if within a month I do not render you great service, punish me as you think fit.' I reply that to me all this appears very just; and that many among us would even not trust him so long as his family remain in the mountains and are not in our hands as hostages; and that I will do everything possible to collect the prisoners on our frontier; that I have no power under our laws to give him money for the ransom of his family in addition to the sum he may himself be able to raise, but that I may perhaps find some other means of helping him. After that I told him frankly that in my opinion Shamil would not in any case give up the family,and that Shamil might tell him so straight out and promise him a full pardon and his former posts, but threaten threaten if Hadji Murád did not return, to kill his mother; his wives, and his six children; and I asked him whether he could say frankly what he would do if he received such an announcement from Shamil. He lifted his eyes and arms to heaven, and said that everything is in God's hands, but that he would never surrender to his foe; for he is certain Shamil would not forgive him, and he would therefore not have long to live. As to the destruction of his family, he did not think Shamil would act so rashly: firstly, to avoid making him a yet more desperate and dangerous foe; and secondly, because there were many people, and even very influential people, in Daghestan, who would dissuade Shamil from such a course. Finally, he repeated several times that whatever God might decree for him in the future, he was at present interested in nothing but his family's ransom; and he implored me, in God's name to help him to and allow him to return to the neighborhood of the Chechnya, where he could, with the help and consent of our commanders, have some intercourse with his family and regular news of their condition; and of the best means to liberate them. He said that many people, and even some *Naibs* in that part of the enemy's territory, were more or less attached to him and that among the whole of the population already subjugated by Russia, or neutral it would be easy with our help to establish relations very useful for the attainment of the aim which gives him no peace day or night, and the attainment of which would set him at ease and make it possible for him to act for our good and win our confidence.

"He asks to be sent back to Grozny with a convoy of twenty or thirty picked Cossacks, who would serve him as a protection against foes and us as a guarantee of his good faith.

"You will understand, dear Prince, that I have been much perplexed by all this, for do what I will, a great responsibility rests on me. It would be in the highest degree rash to trust him entirely, yet in order to deprive him of all means of escape we should have to lock; him up, and in my opinion that would be both unjust and impolitic. A measure of that kind, the news of which would soon spread over the whole of Daghestan, would do us great harm by keeping back those (and there are many such), who are now inclined more or less openly to oppose Shamil and who are keenly watching to see how we treat the Imam's bravest and most adventurous officer now that he has found himself obliged to place himself in our hands. If we treat Hadji Murád as a prisoner, all the good effect of the situation will be lost. Therefore I think that I could not act otherwise than as I have done, though at the same time I feel that I may be accused of having made a great mistake if Hadji Murád should take it into his head to escape again. In the service, and especially in a complicated situation such as this, it is difficult, not to say impossible, to follow any one straight path without risking mistakes, and without accepting responsibility; but once a path seems to be the right one I must follow it, happen what may.

"I beg of you, dear Prince, to submit this to his Majesty the Emperor for his consideration; and I shall be happy if it pleases our most august monarch to approve my action.

"All that I have written above I have also written to Generals Zavodovsky and Kozlovsky, to guide the latter when communicating direct with Hadji Murád, whom I have warned not to act or go anywhere without Kozlovsky's consent. I also told him that it would be all the better for us if he rode out with our convoy, as otherwise Shamil might spread a rumour that we were keeping him prisoner; but at the same time I made him promise never to go to Vozdvizhensk, because my son, to whom he first surrendered and whom he looks upon as his *kunak* (friend), is not the commander of that place and some unpleasant misunderstanding might easily arise. In any case, Vozdvizhensk lies too near a thickly populated, hostile settlement; which for the intercourse with his friends which he desires, Grozny is in all respects suitable.

"Besides the twenty chosen Cossacks who, at his own request are to keep close to him, I am also sending Captain Loris-Melikov with him—a worthy excellent, and highly intelligence officer who speaks Tartar, and knows Hadji Murád well and apparently enjoys his full confidence. During the ten days that Hadji Murád has spent here, he has, however, lived in the same house with Lieutenant- Colonel Prince Tarkhanof, who is in command of the shoushin District, and is here on business connected with the service. He is a truly worthy man whom I trust entirely. He also has won Hadji Murád's confidence, and through him alone —as he speaks Tartar perfectly— we have discussed the most delicate and secret matters. I have consulted Tarkhanof about Hadji Murád, and he fully agrees with me that it was necessary either to act as I have done, or to put Hadji Murád in prison and guard him in the strictest manner (for if we once treat him badly, he will not be easy to hold), or else to remove him from the country altogether. But these two last measures would not only destroy all the advantage accruing to us from Hadji Murád's quarrel with Shamil, but would inevitably check any growth of the present insubordination, and possible future revolt of the people against Shamil's power. Prince Tarkhanov tells me he himself has no doubt of Hadji Murád's truthfulness, and that Hadji Murád is convinced that Shamil will never forgive him, but would have him executed in spite of any promise of forgiveness. The only thing Tarkhanov has noticed in his intercourse with Hadji Murád that might cause any anxiety, is his attachment to his religion. Tarkhanov does not deny that Shamil might influence Hadji Murád from that side. But as I have already said, he will never persuade Hadji Murád that he will not take his life sooner or later should the latter return to him.

"This, dear Prince, is all I have to tell you about this episode in our affairs here."

CHAPTER XV

The report was dispatched from Tiflis on the 24th of December 1851, and on New Year's Eve a courier, having overdriven a dozen horses and beaten a dozen drivers till the blood came, delivered it to Prince Chernyshov, who at that time was Minister of War; and on the 1st of January 1852 Chernyshov among other papers, took Vorontsóv's report, to the Emperor Nicholas.

Chernyshov disliked Vorontsóv because of the general respect in which the latter was held, and because of his immense wealth; and also because Vorontsóv was a real aristocrat while Chernyshov, after all, was a *parvenu*, but especially because the Emperor was particularly well disposed towards Vorontsóv. Therefore at every opportunity Chernyshov tried to injure Vorontsóv.

When he had last presented the report about Caucasian affairs, he had succeeded in arousing Nicholas's displeasure against Vorontsóv because—through the carelessness of those in command—almost the whole of a small Caucasian detachment had been destroyed by the mountaineers. He now intended to present the steps taken by Vorontsóv in relation to Hadji Murád in an unfavorable light. He wished to suggest to the Emperor that Vorontsóv always protected and even indulged the natives, to the detriment of the Russians; and that he had acted unwisely in allowing Hadji Murád to remain in the Caucasus, for there was every reason to suspect that he had only come over to spy on our means of defense, and that it would therefore be better to transport him to Central Russia; and make use of him only after his family had been rescued from the mountaineers and it had become possible to convince ourselves of his loyalty.

Chernyshov's plan did not succeed, merely because on that New Year's Day Nicholas was in particularly bad spirits, and out of perversity would not have accepted any suggestion whatever from any one, least of all from Chernyshov whom he only tolerated —regarding him as indispensable for the time being, but looking upon him as a blackguard, for Nicholas knew of his endeavors at the trial of the Decembrists[1] to secure the conviction of Zachary Chernyshov, and of his attempt to obtain Zachary's property for himself. So thanks to Nicholas's ill temper Hadji Murád remained in the aucasus, and his

1. The military conspirators who tried to secure a Constitution for Russia in 1825, on the accession of Nichoias

circumstances were not changed as they might have been had Chernyshov presented his report at another time.

* * * * *

It was half- past nine o, clock when, through the mist of the cold morning (the thermometer showed 13 degrees below zero Fahrenheit) Chernyshov's fat, bearded coachman, sitting on the box of a small sledge (like the one Nicholas drove about in) with a sharp-angled, cushion- shaped azure velvet cap on his head, drew up at the entrance of the Winter Palace, and gave a friendly nod to his chum, Prince Dolgoruky's coachman—who having brought his master to the palace, had himself long been waiting outside, in his big coat with the thickly wadded skirts, sitting on the reins and rubbing his numbed hands together. Chernyshov had on a long cloak with a large cap and a fluffy collar of silver beaver, and a regulation three-cornered had with cocks' feathers. He threw back the bearskin apron of the sledge, and carefully disengaged his chilled feet, on which he had no goloshas (he prided himself on never wearing any). Clanking his spurs with an air of bravado, he ascended the carpeted steps and passed through the hall door, which was respectfully opened for him by the porter, and entered the hall. Having thrown off his cloak, which an old Court lackey hurried forward to take, he went to a mirror and carefully removed the hat from his curled wig. Looking at himself in the mirror, he arranged the hair on his temples and the tuft above his forehead with an accustomed movement of his old hands, and adjusted his cross, the shoulder-knots of his uniform, and his large-initialled epaulets, and then went up the gently ascending carpeted stairs, his not very reliable old legs feebly mounting the shallow steps. Passing the Court lackeys in gala livery who stood obsequiously bowing, Chernyshov entered the waiting-room. A newly appointed aide-de-camp of the Emperor's in a shining new uniform with epaulets and shoulder-knots, whose face was still fresh and rosy and who had a small black moustache, and the hair on his temples brushed towards his eyes (Nicholas's fashion) met him respectfully.

Prince Vasili Dolgoruky, Assistant-Minister of War, with an expression of *ennui* on his dull face—which was ornamented with similar whiskers, moustaches, and temple tufts brushed forward like Nicholas's—greeted him.

*"L'empereur?"*said Chernyshov, addressing the aidede- camp and looking inquiringly towards the door leading to the cabinet.

"Sa majeste vient de rentrer,"[2] replied the aide-de-camp, evidently enjoying the sound of his own voice, and stepping so softly and steadily that had a tumbler of water been placed on his head none of it would have been spilt, he approached the door and disappeared, his whole body evincing reverence for the spot he was about to visit he disappeared.

Dolgoruky meanwhile opened his portfolio to see that it contained the necessary papers, while Chernyshov, frowning, paced up and down to restore

2. His majesty has just returned.

the circulation in his numbed feet, and thought over what he was about to report to the Emperor. He was near the door of the cabinet when it opened again and the aide-de-camp, even more radiant and respectful than before, came out and with a gesture invited the minister and his assistant to enter.

The Winter Palace had been rebuilt after the fire some considerable time before this; but Nicholas was still occupying rooms in the upper story. The cabinet in which he received the reports of his ministers and other high officials, was a very lofty apartment with four large windows. A big portrait of the Emperor Alexander I hung on the front wall. Between the windows stood two bureaux. By the walls stood several chairs. In the middle of the room was an enormous writing-table, with an arm-chair before it for Nicholas, and other chairs for those to whom he gave audience.

Nicholas sat at the table in a black coat with shoulder-straps but no epaulets, his enormous body—of which the overgrown stomach was tightly laced in—was thrown back, and he gazed at the newcomers with fixed, lifeless eyes. His long, pale face, with its enormous receding forehead between the tufts of hair which were brushed forward and skilfully joined to the wig that covered his bald patch, was specially cold and stony that day. His eyes, always dim, looked duller than usual; the compressed lips under his upturned moustaches, and his fat freshly-shaven cheeks—on which symmetrical sausage-shaped bits of whiskers had been left—supported by the high collar, and his chin which also pressed upon it, gave to his face a dissatisfied and even irate expression. The cause of the bad mood he was in was fatigue. The fatigue was due to the fact that he had been to a masquerade the night before, and while walking about as was his wont, in his Horse Guards' uniform with a bird on the helmet, among the public which crowded round and timidly made way for his enormous, self-assured figure, he again met the mask who at the previous masquerade, by her whiteness, her beautiful figure, and her tender voice had aroused his senile sensuality. She had then disappeared, after promising to meet him at the next masquerade.

At yesterday's masquerade she had come up to him, and he had not let her go, but had led her to the box specially kept ready for that purpose, where he could be alone with her. Having arrived in silence at the door of the box Nicholas looked round to find the attendant, but he was not there. Nicholas frowned and pushed the door open himself, letting the lady enter first.

"Il y a quelq'un!"[3] said the mask, stopping short.

The box actually was occupied. On the small velvet- covered sofasat, close together, an Uhlan officer and a pretty, fair curly-haired young woman in a domino, who had removed her mask. On catching sight of the angry figure of Nicholas drawn up to its full height, she quickly replaced face with her mask, but the Uhlan officer, rigid with fear, gazed at Nicholas with fixed eyes.

3. There's some one there!

Used as he was to the terror he inspired in others, that terror always pleased Nicholas, and by way of contrast he sometimes liked to astound those plunged in terror by addressing kindly words to them. He did so on this occasion.

"Well, friend!" said he to the officer, rigid with fear, "You are younger than I, and might give up your place to me."

The officer jumped to his feet, and growing first pale and then red and bending almost double, he followed his partner silently out of the box, leaving Nicholas alone with his lady.

She proved to be a pretty, twenty-year-old virgin, the daughter of a Swedish governess. She told Nicholas how when quite a child she had fallen in love with him from his portraits; how she adored him and had made up her mind to attract his attention at any cost. Now she had succeeded, and wanted nothing more—so she said.

The girl was taken to the place where Nicholas usually had rendezvous with women, and there he spent more than an hour with her.

When he returned to his room that night and lay on the hard narrow bed about which he prided himself, and covered himself with the cloak which he considered to be (and spoke of as being) as famous as Napoleon's hat, it was a long before he could fall asleep. He thought now of the frightened and elated expression on that girl's fair face, and now of the full, powerful shoulders of his regular mistress, Nelidova, and he compared the two. That profligacy in a married man was a bad thing did not once enter his head, and he would have been greatly surprised had anyone censured him for it. Yet though convinced that he had acted properly, some kind of unpleasant after-taste remained, and to stifle that feeling he dwelt on a thought that always tranquilized him—the thought of his own greatness.

Though he had fell asleep so late, he rose before eight, and after attending to his toilet in the usual way— rubbing his big well-fed body all over with ice—and saying his prayers (repeating those he had been used to from childhood—the prayer to the Virgin, the apostles' Creed, and the Lord's Prayer, without attaching any kind of meaning to the words he uttered), he went out through the smaller portico of the palace onto the embankment in his military cloak and cap.

On the embankment he met a student in the uniform of the School of Jurisprudence, who was as enormous as himself. On recognizing the uniform of that school, which he disliked for its freedom of thought, Nicholas frowned, but the stature of the student and the painstaking manner in which he drew himself up and saluted, ostentatiously sticking out his elbow, mollified his displeasure.

"Your name?" said he.

"Polosatov, your Imperial Majesty." "........fine fellow!"

The student continued to stand with his hand lifted to his hat.

Nicholas stopped.

"Do you wish to enter the army?"

"Not at all, your Imperial Majesty."

"Blockhead!" And Nicholas turned away and continued his walk, and began uttering aloud the first words that came into his head.

"Kopervine...Kopervine—" he repeated several times

(it was the name of yesterday's girl). "Horrid ... horrid—"He did not think of what he was saying, but stifled his feelings by listening to it.

"Yes, what would Russia be without me?" said he, feeling his former dissatisfaction returning. "What would—not Russia alone but Europe be, without me?" and calling to mind the weakness and stupidity of his brother-in-law the King of Prussia, he shook his head.

As he was returning to the small portico, he saw the carriage of Helena Pavlovna,[4] with a red-liveried footman, approaching the Saltykov entrance of the palace.

Helena Pavlovna was to him the personification of that futile class of people who discussed not merely science and poetry, but even the ways of governing men: imagining that they could govern themselves better than he, Nicholas, governed them! He knew that however much he crushed such people they reappeared again and again, and he recalled his brother, Michael Pavlovich, who had died not long before. A feeling of sadness and vexation came over him and with a dark frown he again began whispering the first words that came into his head, which he only ceased doing when he re-entered the palace.

On reaching his apartments he smoothed his whiskers and the hair on his temples and the wig on his bald patch, and twisted his mustaches upwards in front of the mirror, and then went straight to the cabinet in which he received reports.

He first received Chernyshov, who at once saw by his face, and especially by his eyes, that Nicholas was in a particularly bad humour that day, and knowing about the adventure of the night before he understood the cause. Having coldly greeted him and invited him to sit down, Nicholas fixed on him a lifeless gaze. The first matter Chernyshov reported upon was a case of embezzlement by commissariat officials; the next was the movement of troops on the Prussian frontier; then came a list of rewards to be given at the New Year to some people omitted from a former list; then Vorontsóv's report about Hadji Murád; and lastly some unpleasant business concerning an attempt by a student of the Academy of Medicine on the life of a professor.

---

4. Widow of Nicholas's brother Michael: a clever, well-educated woman, interested in science, art, and public affairs.

Nicholas heard the report of the embezzlement silently with compressed lips, his large white hand—with one ring on the fourth finger—stroking some sheets of paper, and his eyes steadily fixed on Chernyshov's forehead and on the tuft of hair above it.

Nicholas was convinced that everybody stole. He knew he would have to punish the commissariat officials now, and decided to send them all to serve in the ranks, but he also knew that this would not prevent those who succeeded them from acting in the same way. It was a characteristic of officials to steal, but it was his duty to punish them for doing so, and tired as he was of that duty he conscientiously performed it.

"It seems there is only one honest man in Russia!" said he.

Chernyshov at once understood that this one honest man was Nicholas himself, and smiled approvingly.

"It looks like it, your Imperial Majesty," said he.

"Leave it—I will give a decision," said Nicholas, taking the document and putting it on the left side of the table.

Then Chernyshov reported the rewards to be given and about moving the army on the Prussian frontier.

Nicholas looked over the list and struck out some names, and then briefly and firmly gave orders to move two divisions to the Prussian frontier. He could not forgive the King of Prussia for granting a Constitution to his people after the events of 1848, and therefore, while expressing most friendly feelings to his brother-in-law in letters and conversation, he considered it necessary to keep an army near the frontier in case of need. He might want to use these troops to defend his brother-inlaw's throne if the people of Prussia rebelled (Nicholas saw a readiness for rebellion everywhere) as he had used troops to suppress the rising in Hungary a few years previously. they were also of use to give more weight and influence to such advice as he gave to the King of Prussia.

"Yes—what would Russia be like now if it were not for me?" he again thought.

"Well, what else is there?" said he.

"A courier from the Caucasus," said Chernyshov, and he reported what Vorontsóv had written about Hadji Murád's surrender.

Dear me !" said Nicholas. "Well, It's a good beginning!"

"Evidently the plan devised by your Majesty begins to bear fruit," said Chernyshov.

This approval of his strategic talents was particularly pleasant to Nicholas because, though he prided himself upon them, at the bottom of his heart he knew that they did not really exist, and he now desired to hear more detailed praise of himself.

"How do you mean?" he asked.

"I understand it this way that if your Majesty's plans had been adopted long ago before, and we had moved forward slowly and steadily, cutting down forests and destroying the supplies of food, the Caucasus would have been subjugated long ago. I attribute Hadji Murád's surrender entirely to his having come to the conclusion that they can hold out no longer."

"True," said Nicholas.

Although the plan of a gradual advance into the enemy's territory by means of felling forests and destroying the food supplies was Ermolov's and Velyaminov's plan, and was quite contrary to Nicholas's own plan of seizing Shamil's place of residence and destroying that nest of robbers—which was the plan on which the dargo expedition in 1845 (that cost so many lives) had been undertaken—Nicholas nevertheless attributed to himself also the plan of a slow advance and a systematic felling of forests and devastation of the country. It would seem that to believe the plan of a slow movement by felling forests and destroying food supplies his own would have necessitated hiding the fact that he had insisted on quite contrary operations in 1845. But he did not hide it and was proud of the plan of the 1845 expedition as well as of the plan of a slow advance—though evidently the two were contrary to one another. Continual brazen flattery from everybody round him in the teeth of obvious facts had brought him to such a state that he no longer saw his own inconsistencies or measured his actions and words by reality, logic, or even simple common sense; but was quite convinced that all his orders, however senseless, unjust, and mutually contradictory they might be, became reasonable, just, and mutually accordant simply because he gave them. His decision in the case next reported to him—that of the student of the Academy of Medicine—was of the that senseless kind.

The case was as follows: A young man who had twice failed in his examinations was being examined a third time, and when the examiner again would not pass him, the young man whose nerves were deranged, considering this to be an injustice, seized a pen-knife from the table in a paroxysm of fury, and rushing at the professor inflicted on him several trifling wounds.

"What's his name?" asked Nicholas.

"Bzhezovsky."

"A Pole?"

"Of Polish descent and a roman Catholic," answered Chernyshov.

Nicholas frowned. He had done much evil to the Poles. To justify that evil he had to feel certain that all Poles were rascals, and he considered them to be such and hated them in proportion to the evil he had done them.

"Wait a little," he said, closing his eyes and bowing his head.

Chernyshov, having more than once heard Nicholas say so, knew that when the Emperor had to take a decision it was only necessary for him to concentrate his attention for a few moments and the spirit moved him, and the best possible decision presented itself as though an inner voice had told him what to do. He was now thinking how most fully to satisfy the feeling of hatred against the Poles which this incident had stirred up within him, and the inner voice suggested the following decision. He took the report and in his large handwriting wrote on its margin with three orthographical mistakes:

"Diserves deth, but, thank God, we have no capitle punishment, and it is not for me to introduce it. Make him fun the gauntlet of a thousand men twelve times.—Nicholas."

He signed, adding his unnaturally huge flourish.

Nicholas knew that twelve thousand strokes with the regulation rods were not only certain death with torture, but were a superfluous cruelty, for five thousand strokes were sufficient to kill the strongest man. But it pleased him to be ruthlessly cruel and it also pleased him to think that we have abolished capital punishment in Russia.

Having written his decision about the student, he pushed it across to Chernyshov.

"There," he said, "read it."

Chernyshov read it, and bowed his head as a sign of respectful amazement at the wisdom of the decision.

"Yes, and let all the students be present on the drill ground at the punishment," added Nicholas.

"It will do them good! I will abolish this revolutionary spirit and will tear it up by the roots!" he thought.

"It shall be done," replied Chernyshov; and after a short pause he straightened the tuft on his forehead and returned to the Caucasian report.

"What do you command me to write in reply to Prince Vorontsóv's dispatch?"

"To keep firmly to my system of destroying the dwellings and food supplies in Chechnya and to harass them by raids." answered Nicholas.

"And what are your Majesty's commands with reference to Hadji Murád?" asked Chernyshov.

"Why, Vorontsóv writes that he wants to make use of him in the Caucasus."

"Is it not dangerous?" said Chernyshov, avoiding Nicholas's gaze. "Prince Vorontsóv is I am afraid too confiding,."

"And you—what do you think?" asked Nicholas sharply, detecting Chernyshov's intention of presenting Vorontsóv's decision in an unfavourable light.

"Well, I should have thought it would be safer to deport him to Central Russia."

"You would have thought!" said Nicholas ironically. "But I don't think so, and agree with Vorontsóv. Write to him accordingly."

"It shall be done," said Chernyshov, rising and bowing himself out.

Dolgoruky also bowed himself out, having during the whole audience only uttered a few words (in reply to a question from Nicholas) about the movement of the army.

After Chernyshov, Nicholas received Bibikov, General-Governor of the Western Provinces. Having expressed his approval of the measures taken by Bibikov against the mutinous peasants who did not wish to accept the orthodox Faith, he ordered him to have all those who did not submit tried by court-martial. that was equivalent to sentencing them to run the gauntlet. He also ordered the editor of a newspaper to be sent to serve in the ranks of the army for publishing information about the transfer of several thousand State peasants to the imperial estates.

"I do this because I consider it necessary," said Nicholas, "and I will not allow it to be discussed."

Bibikov saw the cruelty of the order concerning the Uniate[5] peasants and the injustice of transferring State peasants (the only free peasants in Russia in those days) to the Crown, which meant making them serfs of the Imperial family. But it was impossible to express dissent. Not to agree with Nicholas's decisions would have meant the loss of that brilliant position which it had cost Bibikov forty years to attain, and which he now enjoyed; and he therefore submissively bowed his dark head (already touched with grey) to indicate his submission and his readiness to fulfil the cruel insensate, and dishonest supreme will.

Having dismissed Bibikov, Nicholas with a sense of duty well fulfilled, stretched himself, glanced at the clock, and went to get ready to go out. Having put on a uniform with epaulets, orders, and a ribbon, he went out into the reception hall where more than a hundred persons—men in uniforms and women in elegant low-necked dresses, all standing in the places assigned to them—awaited his arrival with agitation.

He came out to them with a lifeless look in his eyes, his chest expanded, his stomach bulging out above and below its bandages, and feeling everybody's gaze tremulously and obsequiously fixed upon him he assumed an even more triumphant air. When his eyes met those of people he knew, remembering who was who, he stopped and addressed a few words to them sometimes in Russian and sometimes in French, and transfixing them with his cold glassy eye, listened to what they said.

---

5. The Uniates acknowledge the pope of Rome, though in other respects they are in accord with the Orthodox Russo-Greek Church.

Having received all the New year congratulations he passed on to church, God, through His servants the priests, greeted and praised Nicholas just as worldly people did; and weary as he was of these greetings and praises Nicholas duly accepted them. All this was as it should be, because the welfare and happiness of the whole world depended on him, and though the matter wearied still not refuse the universe his assistance.

When at the end of the service the magnificently arrayed deacon, his long hair crimped and carefully combed, began the chant "Many Years," which was heartily caught up by the splendid choir, Nicholas looked round and noticed Nelidova, with her fine shoulders, standing by a window, and he decided the comparison with yesterday's girl in her favour.

After Mass he went to the empress and spent a few minutes in the bosom of his family, joking with the children and his wife. then passing through the Hermitage,[6] he visited the Minister of the Court, Volkonsky, and among other things ordered him to pay out of a special fund a yearly pension to the mother of yesterday's girl. From there he went for his customary drive.

Dinner that day was served in the Pompeian Hall. Besides the younger ons of Nicholas and Michael there were also invited Baron Lieven, Count Rzihevsky, Dolgoruky, the Prussian Ambassador, and the King of Prussia's aide-de-camp.

While waiting for the appearance of the Emperor and Empress an interesting conversation took place between Baron Lieven and the Prussian Ambassador concerning the disquieting news from Poland.

"La Pologne et le Caucases, ce sont les deux cauteres de la Russie,[7]" said Lieven. "Il nous faut 100,000 hommes a peu pres, dans chaqu'un de ces deux pays."

The Ambassador expressed a fictitious surprise that it should be so.

"Vous dites, la Pologne—"[8] began the Ambassador.

"Oh, oui, c'etait un coup de maitre de Metternich de nous en avoir laisse l'embarras... "

At this point the Empress, with her trembling head and fixed smile, entered followed by Nicholas.

At dinner Nicholas spoke of Hadji Murád's surrender, and said that the war in the Caucasus must now soon come to an end in consequence of the measures he was taking to limit the scope of the mountaineers, by felling their forests and by his system of erecting a series of small forts.

---

6. A celebrated museum and picture gallery in St. Prtersburg , adjoining the Winter Palace.
7. " Poland and the Caucasus are Russia's two sores. we need about 100,000 men in each of those two countries.
8. " You say that Poland—" oh yes, it was a master stroke of Metternich's to leave us the bother of it..."

The Ambassador, having exchanged a rapid glance with the aide-de-camp—to whom he had only that morning spoken about Nicholas's unfortunate weakness for considering himself a great strategist—warmly praised this plan which once more demonstrated Nicholas's great strategic ability.

After dinner Nicholas drove to the ballet, where hundreds of women marched round in tights and scant clothing. One of the specially attracted him, and he had the German ballet-master sent for, and gave orders that a diamond ring should be presented to him .

The next day when Chernyshov came with his report, Nicholas again confirmed his order to Vorontsóv—that now that Hadji Murád had surrendered, the Chechens should be more actively harassed than ever and the cordon round them tightened.

Chernyshov wrote in that sense to Vorontsóv; and another courier, overdriving more horses and bruising the faces of more drivers, galloped to Tiflis.

CHAPTER XVI

In obedience to this command of Nicholas a raid was immediately made in Chechnya that same month, January 1852.

The detachment ordered for the raid consisted of four infantry battalions, two companies of Cossacks, and eight guns. The column marched along the road; and on both sides of it in a continuous line, now mounting, now descending, marched *jagers* in high boots, sheepskin coats, and tall caps, with rifles on their shoulders and cartridges in their belts.

As usual when marching through a hostile country, silence was observed as far as possible. Only occasionally the guns jingled, jolting across a ditch, or an artillery horse, snorted or neighed, not understanding that silence was ordered, shorted or neighed or an angry commander shouted in a hoarse subdued voice to his subordinates that the line was spreading out too much or marching too near or too far from the column. Only once was the silence broken, when, from a bramble patch between the line and the column, a gazelle with a white breast and grey back jumped out followed by a buck of the same colour with small backward-curving horns. Doubling up their forelegs at each big bound they took, the beautiful timid creatures came so close to the column that some of the soldiers rushed after them, laughing and shouting, intending to bayonet them, but the gazelles turned back, slipped through the line of *Jigers*, and pursued by a few horsemen and the company's dogs, fled like birds to the mountains.

It was still winter, but towards noon, when the column (which had started early in the morning) had gone three miles, the sun had risen high enough and was powerful enough to make the men quite hot, and its rays were so bright that it was painful to look at the shining steel of the bayonets or at the reflections—like little suns—on the brass of the cannons.

The clear rapid stream the detachment had just crossed lay behind, and in front were tilled fields and meadows in shallow valleys. Further in front were the dark mysterious forest-clad hills with crags rising beyond them, and further still on the lofty horizon were the ever-beautiful ever-changing snowy peaks that played with the light like diamonds.

In a black coat and tall cap, shouldering his sword, at the head of the 5th Company, marched Butler, a tall handsome officer ho had recently exchanged from the Guards. He was filled with a buoyant sense of the joy of living, and also of the danger of death, and with a wish for action, and the consciousness of being part of an immense whole directed by a single will. This was his second time he was going into action and he thought how in a moment they would be fired at, and he would not only not stoop when the shells flew overhead, nor heed the whistle of the bullets, but would carry his head even more erect than before, and would look round at his comrades and the soldiers with smiling eyes, and begin to talk in a perfectly calm voice about quite other matters.

The detachment turned off the good road on to a little-used one that crossed a stubbly maize field, and it was drawing near the forest when—they could not see whence—with an ominous whistle, a shell flew past amid the baggage wagons, and tore up the ground in the field by the roadside.

"It's beginning," said Butler with a bright smile to a comrade who was walking beside him.

And so it was. After the shell, from under the shelter of the forest appeared a thick crowd of mounted Chechens appeared with their banners. In the midst of the crowd could be seen a large green banner, and an old and very far-sighted sergeant-major informed the short-sighted Butler that Shamil himself must be there. The horsemen came down the hill and appeared to the right, at the highest part of the valley nearest the detachment, and began to descend. A little general in a thick black coat and tall cap rode up to Butler's company on his ambler, and ordered him to the right to encounter the descending horsemen. Butler quickly led his company in the direction indicated, but before he reached the valley he heard two cannon shots behind him. He looked round: two clouds of grey smoke had risen above two cannon and were spreading along the valley. The mountaineers' horsemen—who had evidently not expected to meet artillery—retired. Butler's company began firing at them, and the whole ravine was filled with the smoke of powder. Only higher up above the ravine could the mountaineers be seen hurriedly retreating, though still firing back at the Cossacks who pursued them. The company followed the mountaineers further, and on the slope of a second ravine came in view of an *aoul.*

Following the Cossacks, Butler and his company entered the *aoul* at a run. The soldiers were ordered to burn the corn and the hay as well as the *sáklya*s, and the whole *aoul* was soon filled with pungent smoke amid which the soldiers rushed about dragging out of the *sáklya*s what they could find, and above all catching and shooting the fowls the mountaineers had not been able to take away with them.

The officers sat down at some distance beyond the smoke, and lunched and drank. The sergeant-major brought them some honeycombs on a board. There was no sigh of any Chechens and early in the afternoon the order was given to retreat. The companies formed into a column behind the *aoul* and Butler happened to be in the rearguard. As soon as they started Chechens appeared, and following the detachment, fired at it.

When the detachment came out into an open space, the mountaineers pursued it on further. Not one of Butler's company had been wounded, and he returned in a most happy and energetic mood. When after fording the same stream it had crossed in the morning,[1] the detachment spread over the maize fields and the meadows, the singers of each company came forward and songs filled the air.

"Verry diff'rent, very diff'rent, *jagers* are, *jagers* are!" sang Butler's singers, and his horse stepped merrily to the music. Trezorka, the shaggy grey dog of the company, with his tail curled up with an air of responsibility like a commander. Butler felt buoyant, calm, and joyful. War presented itself to him as consisting only in his exposing himself to danger and to possible death, thereby gaining rewards and the respect of his comrades here, as well as of his friends in Russia. Strange to say, his imagination never pictured the other aspect of war: the death and wounds of the soldiers, officers, and mountaineers. To retaint his poetic conception he even unconsciously avoided looking at the dead and wounded. So that day, when we had three dead and twelve wounded, he passed by a corpse lying on its back and did not stop to look, seeing only with one eye the strange position of the waxen hand and a dark red spot on the head and didn't stop to look. The hillsmen appeared to him only a mounted *dzhigits* from whom he had to defend oneself.

"You see, my dear sir," said his major in an interval between two songs, "it's not as it is with you in Petersburg—'Eyes right! Eyes left!' Here we have done our job, and now we go home and Masha will set a pie and some nice cabbage soup before us. That's life—don't you think so?—Now then! *As the Dawn Was Breaking!*" He called for his favourite song.

There was no wind, the air was fresh and clear and so transparent that the snow hills nearly a hundred miles away seemed quite near, and in the intervals between the songs the regular sound of the footsteps and the jingle of the guns was heard as a background on which each song began and ended. The song that was being sung in Butler's company was composed by a cadet in honour of the regiment, and went to a dance tune. The chorus was: "Verry diff'rent, very diff'rent, *jagers* are, *jagers* are!"

Butler rode beside the officer next in rank above him, Major Petrov, with whom he lived and he felt he could not be thankful enough to have exchanged from the Guards and come to the Caucasus. His chief reason for exchanging was that he had lost all he had at cards and was afraid that if he remained there he would be unable to resist playing though he had nothing more to lose. Now all this was over, his life was quite changed and was such a pleasant and brave one! He forgot that he was ruined, and forgot his unpaid debts. The Caucasus, the war, the soldiers, the officers—those tipsy, brave, good-natured fellows and Major Petrov himself, all seemed so delightful that sometimes it appeared

1. Each regiment had a choir of singers.

too good to be true that he was not in Petersburg—in a room filled with tobacco smoke, turning down the corners of cards and gambling, hating the holder of the bank, and feeling a dull pain in his head—but was really here in this glorious region among these brave Caucasians.

The major and the daughter of a surgeon's orderly, formerly known as Masha, but now generally called by the more respectful name of Marya Dmitrievna, lived together as man and wife. Mary Dmitrievna was a handsome, fair-haired, very freckled childless woman of thirty. Whatever her past may have been she was now the major's faithful companion and looked after him like a nurse—a very necessary matter, since he often drank himself into oblivion.

When they reached the fort everything happened as the major had foreseen. Mary Dmitrievna gave him and Butler, and two other officers of the detachment who had been invited, a nourishing and tasty dinner, and the major ate and drank till he was unable to speak, and then went off to his room to sleep.

Butler,tired but contented, having drunk rather more chikhir wine than was good for him, went to his bedroom, tired but contented, and hardly had time to undress before placing his hand under his handsome cusly head, he fell into a sound, dreamless, and unbroken sleep.

CHAPTER XVII

The *aoul* which had been destroyed was that in which Hadji Murád had spent the night before he went over to the Russians. Sado, and his family had left the *aoul* on the approach of the Russian detachment; and when he returned he found his *sáklya* in ruins—the roof fallen in, the door and the posts supporting the penthouse burned, and the interior filthy. His son, the handsome bright-eyed boy who had gazed with such ecstasy at Hadji Murád, was brought dead to the mosque on a horse covered with a *burka;* He had been stabbed in the back with a bayonet. the dignified woman who had served Hadji Murád when he was at the house now stood over her son's body, her smock torn in front, her withered old breasts exposed, her hair down, and she dug her nails into her face till it bled, and wailed incessantly. Sado, taking a pickaxe and spade, had gone with his relatives to dig a grave for his son. The old grandfather sat by the wall of the ruined *sáklya* cutting a stick and gazing solidly in front of him. He had only just returned from the apiary. The two stacks of hay there had been burnt, the apricot and cherry trees he had planted and reared were broken and scorched, and worse still all the beehives and bees were burnt. The wailing of the women and the little children, who cried with their mothers, mingled with the lowing of the hungry cattle for whom there was no food. The bigger children, did not play, but followed their elders with frightened eyes. The fountain was polluted, evidently on purpose, so that the water could not be used. The mosque was polluted in the same way, and the Mullah and his assistants were cleaning it out. No one spoke of hatred of the Russians. The feeling experienced by all the Chechens, from the youngest to the oldest, was stronger than hate. It was not hatred, for they did not regard those Russian dogs as human beings; but it was such repulsion, disgust, and perplexity at the senseless cruelty of these creatures, that the desire to exterminate them—like the desire to exterminate rats, poisonous spiders, or wolves—was as natural an instinct as that of self-preservation.

The inhabitants of the *aoul* were confronted by the choice of remaining there and restoring with frightful effort what had been produced with such labor and had been so lightly and senselessly destroyed, facing every moment the possibility of a repetition of what had happened; or to submit to the Russians—contrary to their religion and despite the repulsion and contempt they felt to submit to the Russians. The old men prayed, and unanimously decided to send envoys to Shamil asking him for help. Then they immediately set to work to restore what had been destroyed.

CHAPTER XVIII

On the morning after the raid, not very early, Butler left the house by the back porch meaning to take a stroll and a breath of fresh air before breakfast, which he usually had with Petrov. The sun had already risen above the hills and it was painful to look at the brightly lit-up white walls of the houses on the right side of the street; but then as always it was cheerful and soothing to look to the left, at the dark receding and ascending forest-clad hills and at the dim line of snow peaks, which as usual pretended to be clouds. Butler looked at these mountains, inhaling deep breaths and rejoiced that he was alive, that it was just he himself that was alive, and that he lived in this beautiful place.

He was also rather pleased that he had behaved so well in yesterday's affair both during the advance and especially during the retreat, when things were pretty hot; he was also pleased to remember how Masha (or Mary Dmitrievna), Petrov's mistress, had treated them at dinner and had been particularly nice and simple with everybody, but specially kind—as he thought—to him.

Mary Dmitrievna with her thick plait of hair, her broad shoulders, her high bosom, and the radiant smile on her kindly freckled face, involuntarily attracted Butler, who was a healthy young bachelor. It sometimes even seemed to him that she wanted him; but he considered that that would be doing his good-natured simple-hearted comrade and he maintained a simple, respectful attitude towards her, and was pleased with himself for so doing .

He was thinking of this when his meditations were disturbed by the tramp of many horses' hoofs along the dusty road in front of him, as if several men were riding that way. He looked up and saw at the end of the street a group of horsemen coming towards him at a walk. In front of a score of Cossacks rode two men: one in a white Circassian coat, with a tall turban on his head; the other an officer in the Russian service, dark, with an aquiline nose, and much silver on his uniform and weapons. The man with the turban rode a fine chestnut horse with mane and tail of a lighter shade, a small head, and beautiful eyes. The officer's was a large, handsome Karabakh horse. Butler, a lover of horses, immediately recognised the great strength of the first horse and stopped to learn who these people were.

The officer addressed him. "This the house of commanding officer?" he asked, his foreign accent and his words betraying his foreign origin.

Butler replied that it was. "And who is that?" he added, coming nearer to the officer and indicating the man with the turban.

"That Hadji Murád. He come here to stay with the commander," said the officer.

Butler knew about Hadji Murád and about his having come over to the Russians, but he had not at all expected to see him here in this little fort. Hadji Murád gave him a friendly look.

"Good day, *Kotkildy,*" said Butler, repeating the Tartar greeting he had learnt.

"Saubul!" ("Be well!") replied Hadji Murád, nodding. He rode up to Butler and held out his hand, from two fingers of which hung his whip.

"Are you the chief?" he asked.

"No, the chief is in here. I will go and call him," said Butler addressing the officer, and he went up the steps and pushed the door. But the door of the visitors' entrance-as Mary Dmitrievna called it, was locked, and as it still remained closed after he had knocked, Butler went round to the back door. He called his orderly but received no reply; and finding neither of the two orderlies; he went into the kitchen, where Mary Dmitrievna— flushed with a kerchief tied round her head and her sleeves rolled up on her plump white arms—was rolling pastry, white as her hands, and cutting it into small pieces to make pies of.

"Where have the orderlies gone to?" asked Butler.

"Gone to drink," replied Mary Dmitrievna.

"What do you want?"

"To have the front door opened. You have a whole horde of mountaineers in front of your house. Hadji Murád has come!"

"Invent something else!" said Mary Dmitrievna, smiling.

"I am not joking, he is really waiting by the porch!"

"Is it really true?" said she.

"Why should I wish to deceive you? Go and see, he's just at the porch!"

"Dear me, here's a go!" said Mary Dmitrievna pulling down her sleeves and putting up her hand to feel whether the hairpins in her thick plait were all in order. "Then I will go and wake Ivan Matveich."

"No, I'll go myself. and you Bondarenko, go and open the door," said he to Petrov's orderly who had just appeared.

"Well, so much the better!" said Mary Dmitrievna and returned to her work.

When he heard that Hadji Murád had come to his house, Ivan Matveich Petrov, the major, who had already heard that Hadji Murád was in Grozny, was not at all surprised. Sitting up in bed he rolled a cigarette, lit it, and began to dress, loudly clearing his throat, and grumbling at the authorities who had sent "that devil" to him.

When he was ready, he told his orderly to bring him some medicine. The orderly knew that "medicine" meant vodka, and brought some.

"There is nothing so bad as mixing," muttered the major when he had drunk the vodka and taken a bite of rye bread. "Yesterday I drank a little chikhir and now I have a headache... Well, I'm ready," he added, and went to the parlour, into which Butler had already shown Hadji Murád and the officer who accompanied him.

The officer handed the major orders from the commander of the left flank to the effect that he should receive Hadji Murád, and should allow him to have intercourse with the mountaineers through spies, but was on no account to allow him to leave the fort without a convoy of Cossacks.

Having read the order, the major looked intently at Hadji Murád and again scrutinized the paper. After passing his eyes several times from one to the other in this manner, he at last fixed them on Hadji Murád and said: *"Yakshi, Bek; yakshi!* (very well, sir, very well!) Let him stay here, and tell him I have orders not to let him out —and what is commanded is sacred! Well, Butler, where do you think we'd better lodge him? Shall we put him in the office?"

Butler had not time to answer before Mary Dmitrievna—who had come from the kitchen and was standing in the doorway—said to the major:

"Why? Keep him here! We will give him the guest chamber and the storeroom. Then at any rate he will be within sight," said she, glancing at Hadji Murád; but meeting his eyes she turned quickly away.

"Well, you know, I think Mary Dmitrievna is right," said Butler.

"Now then, now then; get away! Women have no business here," said the major frowning.

During the whole of this discussion Hadji Murád sat with his hand on the hilt of his dagger and a faint smile of contempt on his lips. He said it was all the same to him where he lodged, and that he wanted nothing but what the Sirdar had permitted —namely; to have communication with the mountaineers, and that he therefore wished they should be allowed to come to him.

The Major said this should be done, and asked Butler to entertain the visitors till something could be got for them to eat, and their rooms prepared. Meantime he himself would go across to the office to write what was necessary and to give some orders.

Hadji Murád's relations with his new acquaintances were at once very clearly defined. From the first he was repelled by, and contempt for the Major, to whom he always behaved very haughtily. Marya Dmitrievna, who prepared and served up his food, pleased him particularly. He liked her simplicity and especially the—to him—foreign type of her beauty, and he was influenced by the attraction she felt towards him and unconsciously conveyed. He tried not to look at her or speak to her, but his eyes involuntarily turned towards her and followed her movements. With butler, from their first acquaintance, he immediately made friends and talked much and willingly with him, questioning him about his life, telling him of his own, communicating to him the news the spies brought him of his family's condition, and even consulting him as to how he ought to act.

The news he received through the spies was not good. During the first four days of his stay in the fort they came to see him twice and both times brought bad news.

CHAPTER XIX

Hadji Murád's family had been removed to Vedeno soon after his desertion to the Russians, and were there kept under guard awaiting Shamil's decision. The women—his old mother Patimat and his two wives with their five little children—were kept under guard in the *sáklya* of the officer, Ibrahim Raschid, while Hadji Murád's son Yusuf, a youth of eighteen, was put in prison—that is, into a pit more than seven feet deep, together with seven criminals, who like himself were awaiting a decision as to their fate.

The decision was delayed, because Shamil was away on a campaign against the Russians.

On 6 January 1852, he returned to Vedeno after a battle, in which according to the Russians he had been vanquished and had fled to Vedeno; but in which according to him and all the *murids* he had been victorious and had repulsed the Russians. In this battle he himself fired his rifle—a thing he seldom did—and drawing his sword would have charged straight at the Russians, had not the *murids* who accompanied him held him back. Two of them were killed on the spot at shamil's side.

It was noon when Shamil, surrounded by a party of *murids* who caracoled around him, firing their rifles and pistols and continually singing *Lya illya il Allah!*—rode up to his place of residence.

All the inhabitants of the large *aoul* were in the street or on their roofs to meet their ruler, and as a sign of triumph they also fired off rifles and pistols. Shamil rode a white Arab steed, which pulled at its bit as it approached the house. The horse had no gold or silver ornaments, its equipment was of the simplest—a delicately worked red leather bridle with a stripe down the middle, metal cup-shaped stirrups, and a red saddle-cloth showing a little from under the saddle. The Imam wore a brown cloth cloak, lined with black fur showing at the neck and sleeves, and was tightly girded round his long thin waist with a black strap which held a dagger. On his head he wore a tall cap with flat crown and black tassel; and round it was wound a white turban, one end of which hung down on his neck. He wore green slippers, and black leggings trimmed with plain braid.

In fact, the Imam nothing bright—no gold or silver—and his tall, erect, powerful figure, clothed in garments without any ornaments, surrounded by *murids* with gold and silver on their clothes and weapons produced on the people just the impression and influence he desired and knew how to produce.

His pale face, framed by a closely trimmed reddish beard, with his small eyes always screwed up, was as immovable as though hewn out of stone. As he rode through the *aoul* he felt the gaze of a thousand eyes turned eagerly on him, but he himself looked at no one.

Hadji Murád's wives had come out into the penthouse with the rest of the inmates of the *sáklya* to see the Imam's entry. Only Patimat, Hadji Murád's old mother, did not go out but remained sitting on the floor of the *sáklya* with her grey hair down, her long arms encircling her thin knees, blinking with her fiery black eyes as she watched the dying embers in the fireplace. She like her son she had always hated Shamil; and now she hated him more than ever and had no wish to see him. Neither did Hadji Murád's son see Shamil's triumphal entry. Sitting in the dark and fetid pit, he heard the firing and singing and endured tortures such as can only be felt by the young who are full of vitality and deprived of freedom. He only saw his unfortunate, dirty, and exhausted fellow-prisoners—embittered, and for the most part filled with hatred of one another. He now passionately envied those who, enjoying fresh air and light and freedom, caracoled on fiery steeds around their chief, shooting and heartily singing: *Lya illyah il Allah!*

When he had crossed the *aoul* Shamil rode into the large courtyard adjoining the inner court where his seraglio was. Two armed Lesghians met him at the open gates of this outer court, which was crowded with people. Some had come from distant parts about their own affairs, some had come with petitions, and some had been summoned by Shamil to be tried and sentenced. As shamil rode in, all respectfully saluted him with their hands on their breasts, some of them kneeling down and remaining on their knees while he rode across the court from the outer to the inner gates. Though he recognised among the people who waited in the court many whom he disliked, and many tedious petitioners who wanted his attention, Shamil passed them all with the same immovable, stony expression on his face, and having entered the inner court dismounted at the penthouse in front of his apartment, to the left of the gate. He was worn out, mentally rather than physically, with the strain of the campaign, for in spite of the public declaration that he had been victorious he knew very well that his campaign had been unsuccessful; that many Chechen *aouls* had been burnt down and ruined, and that the unstable and fickle Chechens were wavering, and those nearest the border line were ready to go over to the Russians.

All this oppressed him, and had to be dealt with; but at that moment he did not wish to think at all. He only desired one thing: rest and the delights of family life, and the caresses of his favourite wife, the black-eyed quick-footed eighteen-year-old black-eyed, quick-footed Aminal, who at that very moment was close at hand behind the fence that divided the inner court and separated the men's from the women's quarters (Shamil felt sure she was there with his other wives, looking through a chink in the fence while he dismounted). but not only was it impossible for him to go to her, he could not even lie down on his feather cushions and rest from his fatigue; he had first of all to perform the mid-day rites for which he had just then not the least inclination, but which as the religious leader of the people-he could not omit, and which moreover, were as necessary to him himself as his daily food. So he performed his ablutions and said his prayers and summoned those who were waiting for him.

The first to enter was Jemal Eddin, his father-in-law and teacher, a tall grey-haired good-looking old man with a beard white as snow and a rosy red face. He said a prayer and began questioning Shamil about the incidents of the campaign and telling him what had happened in the mountains during his absence.

Among events of many kinds—murders connected with blood-feuds, cattle stealing, people accused of disobeying the Tarikat (smoking and drinking wine)—Jemal Eddin related how Hadji Murád had sent men to bring his family over to the Russians, but that this had been detected and the family had been brought to Vedeno, where they were kept under guard and awaited the Imam's decision. In the next room, the guest-chamber,the Elders were assembled to discuss all these affairs, nd Jemal Eddin advised Shamil to finish with them and let them go that same day, as they had already been waiting three days for him.

After eating his dinner—served to him in his room by Zeidat, a dark, sharp-nosed, disagreeable-looking woman whom he did not love but who was his eldest wife—Shamil passed into the guest chamber.

The six old men who made up his council—white, grey, or red-bearded, with tall caps on their heads, some with turbans and some without, wearing new *beshmets* and Circassian coats girdled with straps on which their daggers were suspended—rose to greet him on his entrance. Shamil towered a head above them all. On entering the room he, as well as all the others, lifted his hands, palms upwards, closed his eyes and recited a prayer, and then stroked his face downwards with both hands, uniting them at the end of his beard. Having done this they all sat down, Shamil on a larger cushion than the others, and discussed the various cases before them.

In the case of the criminals the decisions were given according to the Shariat, two were sentenced to have a hand cut off for stealing, one man to be beheaded for murder, and three were pardoned. Then they came to the principal business: how to stop the Chechens from going over to the Russians. To counteract that tendency Jemal Eddin drew up the following proclamation:—

"I wish you eternal peace with God the Almighty!

"I hear that the Russians flatter you and invite you to surrender to them, Do not belive them, and do not surrender, but endure. If ye be not rewarded for it in this life ye shall receive your reward in the life to come. Remember what happened before when they took your arms from you! If God had not brought you to reason then, in 1840, ye would now be soldiers, and your wives would no longer wear trousers and would be dishonoured.

"Judge of the future by the past. It is better to die in enmity with the Russians than to live with the Unbelievers. Endure for a little while, and I will come with the Koran and the sword, and will lead you against the enemy. But now I strictly command you not only to entertain no intention, but not even a thought, of submitting to the Russians!"

Shamil approved this proclamation, signed it, and had it sent out.

After this business they considered Hadji Murád's case. This was of the utmost importance to Shamil. Although he did not wish to admit it, he knew that if Hadji Murád with his agility boldness, and courage, had been with him, what had now happened in Chechnya would not have occurred. It would therefore be well to make it up with Hadji Murád and have the benefit of his services; but as this was not possible it would never do to allow him to help the Russians and therefore he must enticed back and killed. They might accomplish this either by sending a man to Tiflis who would kill him there, or by inducing him to come back and then killing him. The only means of doing the latter was by making use of his family, and especially his son, whom Shamil knew he loved passionately. Therefore they must act through the son.

When the councilors had talked all this over, Shamil closed his eyes and sat silent.

The councillors knew that this meant that he was listening to the voice of the Prophet, who spoke to him and told him what to do.

After five minutes of solemn silence Shamil opened his eyes, and narrowing them more than usual, said:—

"Bring Hadji Murád's son to me."

"He is here," replied Jemal Eddin, and in fact Yusuf, Hadji Murád's son, thin, pale, tattered, and evil-smelling, but still handsome in face and figure, with black eyes that burnt like his grandmother Patimat's, was already standing by the gate of the outside court, waiting to be called in.

Yusuf did not share his father's feelings towards Shamil. He did not know all that had happened in the past, or if he knew it, not having lived through it he still did not understand why his father was so obstinately hostile to Shamil. To him who wanted only one thing— to continue living the easy life that as the Naib's son, he had led in Kuhzakh—it seemed quite unnecessary to be at enmity with Shamil. Out of defiance and a spirit of contradiction to his father he particularly admired Shamil, and shared the ecstatic adoration with which he was regarded in the mountains. With a peculiar feeling of tremulous veneration for the Imam he now entered the guest chamber. As he stopped by the door he met the steady gaze of Shamil's half-closed eyes. He paused for a moment, and then approached Shamil and kissed his large, long-fingered hand.

"Thou art Hadji Murád's son?"

"I am, Imam."

"Thou knowest what he has done?"

"I know, Imam, and deplore it."

"Canst thou write?"

"I was preparing myself to be a Mullah—"

"Then write to thy father that if he will return to me now, before the Feast of Bairam, I will forgive him and everything shall be as it was before; but if not, and if he remains with the Russians"—and Shamil frowned sternly—"I will give thy grandmother, thy mother, and the rest to the different *aouls,* and thee I will behead!"

Not a muscle of Yusuf's face stirred, and he bowed his head to show that he understood Shamil's words.

"Write that and give it to my messenger."

Shamil ceased speaking, and looked at Yusuf for a long time in silence.

"Write that I have had pity on thee and will not kill thee, but will put out thine eyes as I do to all traitors!...Go!"

While in Shamil's presence Yusuf appeared calm, but when he had been led out of the guest chamber he rushed at his attendant, snatched the man's dagger from its sheath, and tried to stab himself; but he was seized by the arms, bound, and led back to the pit.

That evening at dusk after he had finished his evening prayers, Shamil put on a white fur-lined cloak and passed out to the other side of the fence where his wives lived, and went straight to Aminal's room, but he did not find her there. She was with the older wives. Then Shamil, trying to remain unseen, hid behind the door and stood waiting for her. But Aminal was angry with him because he had given some silk stuff to Zeidat and not to her. She saw him come out and go into her room looking for her, and she purposely kept away. She stood a long time at the door of Zeidat's room, laughing softly at Shamil's white figure that kept going in and out of her room.

Having waited for her in vain, Shamil returned to his own apartments when it was already time for the midnight prayers.

CHAPTER XX

Hadji Murád had been a week in the major's house at the fort. Although Mary Dmitrievna quarrelled with the shaggy Khanefi (Hadji Murád had only brought two of his *murids,* Khanefi and Eldár, with him) and had turned him out of her kitchen—for which he nearly killed her—she evidently felt a particular respect and sympathy for Hadji Murád. She now no longer served him his dinner, having handed that duty over to Eldár, but she seized every opportunity of seeing him and rendering him service. She always took the liveliest interest in the negotiations about his family, knew how many wives and children he had, and their ages, and each time a spy came to see him she inquired as best she could into the results of the negotiations.

Butler during that week had become quite friendly with Hadji Murád. Sometimes the latter came to Butler's room, sometimes Butler went to Hadji Murád's: sometimes they conversed by the help of the interpreter, and sometimes they got on as best they could with signs and especially with smiles.

Hadji Murád had evidently taken a fancy to Butler, as could be gathered from Eldár's relations with the latter. When Butler entered Hadji Murád's room, Eldár met him with a pleased smile showing his glittering teeth, and hurried to put down a cushion for him to sit on and to relieve him of his sword if he was wearing one.

Butler also got to know, and became friendly with, the shaggy Khanefi, Hadji Murád's sworn brother. Khanefi knew many mountain songs and sang them well, and to please Butler, Hadji Murád often made Khanefi sing, choosing the songs he considered best. Khanefi had a high tenor voice, and sang with extraordinary clearness and expression. One of the songs Hadji Murád specially liked impressed Butler by its solemnly mournful tone, and he asked the interpreter to translate it.

The subject of the song was the very blood-feud that had existed between Khanefi and Hadji Murád. It ran as follows:—

The earth will dry on my grave,
    Mother, my Mother!
And thou wilt forget me,
And over me rank grass will wave,
    Father, my Father!
Nor wilt thou regret me!

When tears cease thy dark eyes to lave,
    Sister, dear Sister!
No more will grief fret thee!
But thou, my Brother the Elder, wilt never forget,
    With vengeance denied me!
And thou, my Brother the younger, wilt ever regret,
    Till thou liest beside me!
Hotly thou camest, O death-bearing ball that I spurned,
    For thou wast my slave!
And thou, black earth, that battle-steed trampled and churned
        Wilt cover my grave!
"Cold art Thou, O Death, yet I was thy Lord and thy Master!
My body sinks fast to the earth; my Soul to Heaven flies faster.

Hadji Murád always listened to this song with closed eyes and when it ended on a long gradually dying note he always remarked in Russian, —

"Good song! Wise song!"

After Hadji Murád's arrival and Butler's intimacy with him and his *murids,* the poetry of the energetic life of the mountains took a still stronger hold on Butler. He procured for himself a *beshmet*, a Circassian coat and leggings, and imagined himself a mountaineer living the life those people lived.

On the day of Hadji Murád's departure the major invited several officers to see him off. They were sitting, some at the table where Mary Dmitrievna was pouring out tea, some at another table on which stood vodka chikhir, and light refreshments, when Hadji Murád dressed for the journey, came limping with soft rapid footsteps into the room.

They all rose and shook hands with him. The major offered him a seat on the divan, but Hadji Murád thanked him and sat down on a chair by the window.

The silence that followed his entrance did not at all abash him. He looked attentively at all the faces and fixed an indifferent gaze on the tea-table with the *samovar* and refreshments. Petrovsky, a lively officer who now met Hadji Murád for the first time, asked him through the interpreter whether he liked Tiflis.

"Alya!" he replied.

"He says 'Yes'," translated the interpreter.

"What did he like there?"

Hadji Murád said something in reply.

"He liked the theater best of all."

"And how did he like the ball at the house of the commander- in-chief?"

Hadji Murád frowned. "Every nation has its own customs! Our women do not dress in such a way," said he, glancing at Mary Dmitrievna.

"Well, didn't he like it?"

"We have a proverb," said Hadji Murád to the interpreter,

"'The dog gave meat to the ass and the ass gave hay to the dog, and both went hungry,'" and he smiled. "Its own customs seem good to each nation.

The conversation went no farther. Some of the officers took tea, some other refreshments. Hadji Murád accepted the tumbler of tea offered him and put it down before him.

"Won't you have cream and a bun?" asked Mary Dmitrievna, offering them to him. Hadji Murád bowed his head.

"Well, I suppose it is good-bye!" said Butler, touching his knee. "When shall we meet again?"

"Good-bye, good-bye!" said Hadji Murád with a smile, in Russian, . *"Kunak bulug.* Strong *kunak* to thee! Time—*ayda —go!"* and he jerked his head in the direction in which he had to go.

Eldár appeared in the doorway carrying something large and white across his shoulder and a sword in his hand. Hadji Murád beckoned him to and he crossed the room with big strides and handed him a white *búrka* and the sword. Hadji Murád rose, took the *búrka*, threw it over his arm, and saying something to the interpreter handed it to Mary Dmitrievna.

"The interpreter said "He says thou has praised the *búrka*, so accept it."

"Oh, why?" said Mary Dmitrievna blushing.

"It is necessary. Like Adam," said Hadji Murád.

"Well, thank you," said Mary Dmitrievna, taking the *búrka*. "God grant that you rescue your son," she added. "*Ulan yakshi.* Tell him that I wish him success in releasing his son."

Hadji Murád glanced at Mary Dmitrievna and nodded his head approvingly. Then he took the sword from Eldár and handed it to the Major. The Major took it and said to the interpreter,—

"Tell him to take my chestnut gelding. I have nothing else to give him."

Hadji Murád waved his hand in front of his face to show that he did not want anything and would not accept it. Then, pointing first to the mountains and then to his heart, he went out.

Every one followed him as far as the door, while the officers who remained inside the room drew the sword from its scabbard, examined its blade, and decided that it was a real Gurda.[1]

Butler accompanied Hadji Murád to the porch, and then came a very unexpected incident which might have ended fatally for Hadji Murád had it not been for his quick observation, determination, and agility.

---

1. A highly-prized quality of blade

The inhabitants of the Kumukh *aoul,* Tash-Kichu, which was friendly to the Russians, respected Hadji Murád greatly and had often come to the fort merely to look at the famous *Naib*. They had sent messengers to him three days previously to ask him to visit their mosque on the Friday. But the Kumukh princes who lived in Tash-Kichu hated Hadji Murád because there was a blood-feud between them, and on hearing of this invitation they announced to the people that they would not allow him to enter the mosque. The people became excited, and a fight occurred between them and the princes' supporters. The Russian authorities pacified the mountaineers and sent word to Hadji Murád not to go to the mosque.

Hadji Murád did not go and everyone supposed that the matter was settled.

But at the very moment of his departure, when he came out into the porch before which the horses stood's waiting, Arslan Khan's, one of the Kumukh princes and an acquaintance of Butler and the Major-rode up to the house.

When he saw Hadji Murád he snatched a pistol from his belt and took aim, but before he could fire, Hadji Murád in spite of his lameness rushed down from the porch like a cat towards Arslan Khan who fired and missed.

Seizing Arslan Khan's horse by the bridle with one hand, Hadji Murád drew his dagger with the other and shouted something to him in Tartar.

Butler and Eldár both ran at once towards the enemies and caught them by the arms. The Major, who had heard the shot, also came out.

"What do you mean by it, Arslan—starting such a nasty business on my premises?" said he, when he heard what had happened. "It's not right, friend! 'To the foe in the field you need not yield!'—but to start this kind of slaughter in my place—!"

Arslan Khan, a little man with black mustaches, got off his horse pale and trembling, looked angrily at Hadji Murád, and went into the house with the major. Hadji Murád, breathing heavily and smiling, returned to the horses.

"Why did he want to kill him?" Butler asked the interpreter.

"He says it is a law of theirs," the interpreter translated Hadji Murád's reply. "Arslan must avenge a relation's blood and so he tried to kill him."

"And supposing he overtakes him on the road?" asked Butler.

Hadji Murád smiled.

"Well, if he kills me it will prove that such is Allah's will...Good-bye," he said again in Russian, taking his horse by the withers. Glancing round at everybody who had come out to see him off, his eyes rested kindly on Mary Dmitrievna.

"Good-bye, my lass," said he to her. "I thank you."

"God help you—Gold help you to rescue your family!" repeated Mary Dmitrievna.

He did not understand her words, but felt her sympathy for him and nodded to her.

"Mind, don't forget your *kunak,*" said Butler.

"Tell him I am his true friend and will never forget him," answered Hadji Murád to the interpreter, and in spite of his short leg he swung himself lightly and quickly, into the high saddle, barely touching the stirrup, and automatically feeling for his dagger and adjusting his sword. Then, with that peculiarly proud look with which only a Caucasian hill-man sits his horse— as though he were one with it—he rode away from the major's house. Khanefi and Eldár also mounted and having taken a friendly leave of their hosts and of the officers, rode off at a trot, following their *murshid.*

As usual after a departure, those who remained behind began to discuss them.

"Plucky fellow! He rushed at Arslan Khan like a wolf! His face quite changed!"

"But he'll be up to tricks—he's a terrible rogue, I should say," remarked Petrovsky.

"God grant there were more Russian rogues of such a kind!" suddenly put in Mary Dmitrievna with vexation. "He has lived a week with us and we have seen nothing but good from him. He is courteous, wise, and just" she added.

"How did you find that out?"

"Well, I did find it out!"

"She's quite smitten," said the major, who had just entered the room. "and that's a fact!"

"Well, and if I am smitten? What's that to you? Why run him down if he's a good man? Though he's a Tartar he's still a good man!"

"Quite true, Mary Dmitrievna," said Butler, "and you're quite right to take his part!"

CHAPTER XXI

Life in our advanced forts in the Chechen lines went on as usual. Since the events last narrated there had been two alarms when the companies were called out, and militiamen galloped about; but both times the mountaineers who had caused the excitement got away; and once at Vozdvizhensk they killed a Cossack and succeeded in carrying off eight Cossack horses that were being watered. there had been no further raids since the one in which the *aoul* was destroyed, but an expedition on a large scale was expected in consequence of the appointment of a new commander of the left flank, Prince Baryatinsky. He was an old friend of the Viceroy's and had been in command of the Kabarda Regiment. On his arrival at Grozny as commander of the, Left Flank he at once mustered a detachment to continue to carry out the Tsar's commands as communicated by Chernyshov to Vorontsóv. The detachment mustered at Vozdvizhensk left the fort, and took up a position towards Kurín, where the troops were encamped and were felling the forest. Young Vorontsóv lived in a splendid cloth tent, and his wife, Mary Vasilevna, often came to the camp and stayed the night. Baryatinsky's relations with Mary Vasilevna were no secret to anyone, and the officers who were not in the aristocratic set and the soldiers abused her in coarse terms—for her presence in camp caused them to be told off to lie in ambush at night. The mountaineers were in the habit of bringing guns with in range and firing shells at the camp. The shells generally missed their aim, and therefore at ordinary times no special measures were taken to prevent such firing; but now, men were placed in ambush to hinder the mountaineers from injuring or frightening Mary Vasilevna with their cannons. To have to be always lying in ambush at night to save a lady from being frightened, offended and annoyed them; and therefore the soldiers, as well as the officers not admitted to the higher society, called Mary Vasilevna bad names.

Butler, Having obtained leave of absence from his fort, came to the camp to visit some old messmates from the cadet corps and fellow officers of the Kurín regiment who were serving as adjutants and orderly officers. When he first arrived he had a very good time. He put up in Poltorátsky's tent and there met many acquaintances who gave him a hearty welcome. He also called on Vorontsóv, whom he knew slightly, having once served in the same regiment with him. Vorontsóv received him very kindly, introduced him to Prince Baryatinsky, and invited him to the farewell dinner he was giving in honour of General Kozlovsky, who, until Baryatinsky's arrival had been in command of the Left Flank.

The dinner was magnificent. Special tents were erected in a line, and along the whole length of them a table was spread, as for a dinner-party, with dinner services and bottles. Everything recalled life in the Guards in Petersburg. Dinner was served at two o'clock. Kozlovsky sat in the middle on one side. on the other Baryatinsky. At Kozlovsky's right and left hand sat the Vorontsóvs, husband and wife. All along the table on both sides sat the officers of the Kabarda and Kurín regiments. Butler sat next to Poltorátsky and they both chatted merrily and drank with the officers around them. When the roast was served and the orderlies had gone round and filled the champagne glasses, Poltorátsky with real anxiety, said to Butler, —

"Our Kozlovsky will disgrace himself!"

"Why?"

"Why, he'll have to make a speech, and what good is he at that?...Yes not as easy as capturing entrenchments under fire! And with a lady beside him, too, and these aristocrats!"

"Really it's painful to look at him," said the officers to one another. And now the solemn moment had arrived. Baryatinsky rose and lifting his glass, addressed a short speech to Kozlovsky. When he had finished, Kozlovsky—who always had a trick of using the word "how" superfluously—rose and stammeringly began:—

"In compliance with the august will of his Majesty I am leaving you—parting from you, gentlemen,"said he. "But consider me as always remaining among you. The truth of the proverb, how 'One man in the field is no warrior', is well known to you, gentlemen...Therefore, how every reward I have received...how all the benefits showered on me by the great generosity of our sovereign the Emperor...how all my position—how my good name...how everything decidedly...how..."(here his voice trembled) "... how I am indebted to you for it, to you alone, my friends!" The wrinkled face puckered up still more, he gave a sob and tears came into his eyes. "How from my heart I offer you my sincerest, heartfelt gratitude!"

Kozlovsky could not go on but turned round and began to embrace the officers. The princess hid her face in her handkerchief. The prince blinked, with his mouth drawn awry. Many of the officers' eyes grew moist and Butler, who had hardly known Kozlovsky, could also not restrain his tears. He liked all this very much.

Then followed other toasts. Baryatinsky, Vorontsóv, the officers, and the soldiers, healths were drunk and the visitors left the table intoxicated with wine and with the military elation to which they were always so prone. The weather was wonderful, sunny and calm, and the air fresh and bracing. On all sides bonfires crackled and songs resounded. It might have been thought that everybody was celebrating some joyful event. Butler went to Poltorátsky's in the happiest, most emotional mood. Several officers had gathered there, and a card table was set. An adjutant started a bank with a hundred rubles. Two or three times Butler left the tent with his hand gripping the purse in his trousers-pocket, but at last he could resist the temptation no longer, and despite the promise he had given to his brother and to himself not to play, he began to do so. Before an hour was past, very red, perspiring, and soiled with chalk, he was sitting with both elbows on the table and wrote on it—under cards bent for "corners" and "transports— the figures of his stakes. He had already lost so much that he was afraid to count up what was scored against him. But he knew without counting that all the pay he could draw in advance, added to the value of his horse, would not suffice to pay what the adjutant, a stranger to him, had written down against him. He would still have gone on playing, but the adjutant sternly laid down the cards he held in his large clean hands and added up the chalked figures of the score of Butler's losses. Butler, in confusion began to make excuses for being unable to pay the whole of his debt at once, and said he would send it from home. When he said this he noticed that everybody pitied him and that they all—even Poltorátsky—avoided meeting his eye. That was his last evening there. He need only have refrained from playing and gone to the Vorontsóvs who had invited him, and all would have been well, but now it was not only not well—it was terrible.

Having taken leave of his comrades and acquaintances he rode home and went to bed, and slept for eighteen hours as people usually sleep after losing heavily. From the fact that he asked her to lend him fifty kopeks to tip the Cossack who had escorted him, and from his sorrowful looks and short answers, Marya Dmitrievna guessed that he had lost at cards and she reproached the major for having given him leave of absence.

When he woke up at noon next day and remembered the situation he was in he longed again to plunge into the oblivion from which he had just emerged, but it was impossible. Steps had to be taken to repay the four hundred and seventy rubles he owed to the stranger. The first step he took was to write to his brother, confessing his sin and imploring him for the last time, to lend him five hundred roubles on the security of the mill they still owned in common. Then he wrote to a stingy relative asking her to lend him five hundred rubles at whatever rate of interest she liked. Finally he went to the major, knowing that he—or rather Marya Dmitrievna—had some money, and asked him to lend him five hundred roubles.

"I'd let you have them at once," said the major, "but Masha won't! These women are so close-fisted—who the devil can understand them?...And yet you must get out of it somehow, devil take him!...Hasn't that brute the canteen-keeper got something?

"But it was no use trying to borrow from the canteenkeeper, so Butler's salvation could only come from his brother or his stingy relative.

CHAPTER XXII

Not having attained his aim in Chechnya, Hadji Murád returned to Tiflis and went every day to Vorontsóv's; and whenever he could obtain audience he implored the Viceroy to gather together the mountaineer prisoners and exchange them for his family. He said that unless that were done his hands were tied and he could not serve the Russians and destroy Shamil, as he desired to do. Vorontsóv vaguely promised to do what he could, but put it off, saying that he would decide when General Argutinsky reached Tiflis and he could talk the matter over with him.

Then Hadji Murád asked Vorontsóv to allow him to go to live for a while in Nukha, a small town in Transcaucasia, where he thought he could better carry on negotiations about his family with Shamil and with the people who were attached to himself. Moreover Nukha, being a Mohammedan town, had a mosque where he could more conveniently perform the rites of prayer demanded by the Mohammedan law. Vorontsóv wrote to Petersburg about it but meanwhile gave Hadji Murád permission to go to Nukha.

For Vorontsóv and the authorities in Petersburg, as well as for most Russians acquainted with Hadji Murád's history, the whole episode presented itself as a lucky turn in the Caucasian war, or simply as an interesting event. For Hadji Murád it was a terrible crisis in his life—especially latterly. He had escaped from the mountains partly to save himself and partly out of hatred of Shamil, and difficult as this flight had been he had attained his object, and for a time was glad of his success and really devised a plan to attack Shamil but the rescue of his family—which he had thought would be easy to arrange—had proved more difficult than he expected.

Shamil had seized the family and kept them prisoners, threatening to hand the women over to the different *aouls* and to blind or kill the son. Now Hadji Murád had gone to Nukha intending to try, by the aid of his adherents in Daghestan, to rescue his family from Shamil by force or by cunning. The last spy who had come to see him in Nukha informed him that the Avars, devoted to him, were preparing to capture his family and to come over to the Russians with it, but that there were not enough of them and they could not risk making the attempt in Vedeno, where the family was at present imprisoned, but could do so only if the family were moved from Vedeno to some other place— in which case they promised to rescue them on the way.

Hadji Murád sent word to his friends that he would give three thousand rubles for the liberation of his family.

At Nukha a small house of five rooms was assigned to Hadji Murád near the mosque and the Khan's palace. The officers in charge of him, his interpreter, and his henchmen stayed in the same house. Hadji Murád's life was spent in the expectation and reception of messengers from the mountains and in rides he was allowed to take in the neighborhood.

On 24th April, returning from one of these rides, Hadji Murád learnt that during his absence an official had arrived from Tiflis. In spite of his longing to know what message the official had brought him, Hadji Murád, before going into the room where the officer in charge and the official were waiting. This room served him both as drawing room and reception room. The official who had come from Tiflis, Councillor Kirillov, informed Hadji Murád of Vorontsóv's wish that he should come to Tiflis on the 12th to meet General Argutinski.

*"Yakshi!"*said Hadji Murád angrily. The councillor did not please him. "Have you brought money?"

"I have," answered Kirillov.

"For two weeks now," said Hadji Murád, holding up first both hands and then four fingers."Give here!"

"We'll give it you at once," said the official, getting his purse out of his travelling bag. "What does he want with the money?" he went on in Russian, thinking that Hadji Murád would not understand. But Hadji Murád had understood, and glanced angrily at Kirrillov. While getting out the money the councillor, wishing to begin a conversation with Hadji Murád in order to have something to tell Prince Vorontsóv on his return, asked through the interpreter whether he was not feeling dull there. Hadji Murád glanced contemptuously out of the corner of his eye at the fat, unarmed little man dressed as a civilian, and did not reply. The interpreter repeated the question.

"Tell him that I cannot talk with him! Let him give me the money!"and having said this, Hadji Murád sat down at the table ready to count the money.

When Kirillov and had got out the money and arranged it in seven piles of ten gold pieces each (Hadji Murád received of five gold piece daily and pushed them towards Hadji Murád, the latter poured the gold into the sleeve of his Circassian coat, rose, and quite unexpectedly slopped Councillor Kirillov on his bald pate, and turned to go.

The councillor jumped up and ordered the interpreter to tell Hadji Murád that he must not dare to behave like that to him who held a rank equal to that of colonel! The officer in charge confirmed this, but Hadji Murád only nodded to signify that he knew, and left the room.

"What is one to do with him?" said the officer in charge. "He'll stick his dagger into you, that's all! One cannot talk with those devils! I see that he is getting exasperated."

As soon as it began to grow dusk, two spys with hoods covering their faces up to their eyes, came to him from the hills. The officer in charge led them to Hadji Murád's room. One of them was a fleshy, swarthy Tavlinian, the other a thin old man. The news they brought was not cheering. for Hadji Murád's friends who had undertaken to rescue his family now definitely refused to do so, being afraid of Shamil, who threatened to punish with most terrible tortures anyone who helped Hadji Murád. Having heard the messengers he sat with his elbows on his crossed legs, and bowing his turbaned head remained silent a long time.

He was thinking and thinking resolutely. He knew that he was now considering the matter for the last time and that it was necessary to come to a decision. At last he raised his head, gave each of the messengers a gold piece, and said: "Go!"

"What answer will there be?"

"The answer will be as God pleases…Go!"

The messengers rose and went away, and Hadji Murád continued to sit on the carpet leaning his elbows on his knees. He sat thus a long time and pondered.

"What am I to do? To take Shamil at his word and return to him?" he thought. "He is a fox and will deceive me. Even if he did not deceive me it would still be impossible to submit to that red liar. It is impossible…because now that I have been with the Russians he will not trust me," thought Hadji Murád; and he remembered a Tavlinian fable about a falcon who had been caught and lived among men and afterwards returned to his own kind in the hills. He returned, wearing jesses with bells, and the other falcons would not receive him. "Fly back to where they hung those silver bells on thee!" said they. "We have no bells and no jesses." The falcon did not want to leave his home, and remained, but the other falcons did not wish to let him stay there and pecked him to death.

"And they would peck me to death in the same way," thought Hadji Murád. "Shall I remain here and conquer Caucasia for the Russian Tsar and earn renown, titles, riches?"

"That could be done," thought he, recalling his interviews with Vorontsóv and the flattering things the prince had said; "but I must decide at once, or Shamil will destroy my family."

That night he remained awake, thinking.

CHAPTER XXIII

By midnight his decision had been formed. He had decided that he must fly to the mountains, and break into Vedeno with the Avars still devoted to him, and either die or rescue his family. Whether after rescuing them he would return to the Russians or escape to Khunzakh and fight Shamil, he had not made up his mind. All he knew was that first of all he must escape from the Russians into the mountains, and he at once began to carry out his plan.

He drew his black wadded beshmet from under his pillow and went into his henchmen's room. They lived on the other side of the hall. As soon as he entered the hall, the outer door of which stood open, he was at once enveloped by the dewy freshness of the moonlit night and his ears were filled by the whistling and trilling of several nightingales in the garden by the house.

Having crossed the hall he opened the door of his henchmen's room. There was no light there, but the moon in its first quarter shone in at the window. A table and two chairs were standing on one side of the room, and four of his henchmen were lying on carpets or on *búrka*s on the floor. Khanefi slept outside with the horses. Gamzálo heard the door creak, rose, turned round, and saw him. On recognizing him he lay down again, but Eldár, who lay beside him, jumped up and began putting on his *beshmet,* expecting his master's orders. Khan Mahoma and Bata slept on. Hadji Murád put down the *beshmet* he had brought on the table, which it hit with a dull sound, caused by the bold sewn up in it.

"Sew these in too," said Hadji Murád, handing Eldár the gold pieces he had received that day. Eldár took them and at once went into the moonlight, drew a small knife from under his dagger and started unstitching the lining of the *beshmet.* Gamzálo raised himself and sat up with his legs crossed.

"And you, Gamzálo, tell the men to examine the rifles and pistols and get the ammunition ready. Tomorrow we shall go far," said Hadji Murád.

"We have bullets and powder, everything shall be ready," replied Gamzálo, and roared out something incomprehensible. He understood why Hadji Murád had ordered the rifles to be loaded. From the first he had desired only one thing—to slay and stab as many Russians as possible and to escape to the hills—and this desire had increased day by day. Now at last he saw that Hadji Murád also wanted this and he was satisfied.

When Hadji Murád went away Gamzálo roused his comrades, and all four spent the rest of the night examining their rifles, pistols, flints, and accoutrements; replacing what was damaged, sprinkling fresh powder onto the pans, and stoppering with bullets wrapped in oiled rags, packets filled with the right amount of powder for each charge, sharpening their swords and daggers and greasing the blades with tallow.

Before daybreak Hadji Murád again came out into the hall to get water for his ablutions. The songs of the nightingales that had burst into ecstasy at dawn were now even louder and more incessant, while from his henchmen's room, where the daggers were being sharpened, came the regular screech and rasp of iron against stone.

Hadji Murád got himself some water from a tub, and was already at his own door when above the sound of the grinding he heard from his *murids'* room the high tones of Khanefi's voice singing a familiar song. He stopped to listen. The song told of how a *dzhigit,* Hamzad, with his brave followers captured a herd of white horses from the Russians, and how a Russian prince followed him beyond the Terek and surrounded him with an army as large as a forest; and then the song went on to tell how Hamzad killed the horses, entrenched his men behind this gory bulwark, and fought the Russians as long as they had bullets in their rifles, daggers in their belts, and blood in their veins. But before he died Hamzad saw some birds flying in the sky and cried to them:—

Fly on, ye winged ones, fly to our homes!
Tell ye our mothers, tell ye our sisters,
Tell the white maidens, that fighting we died
For Ghazavat! Tell them our bodies
Never will lie and rest in a tomb!
Wolves will devour and tear them to pieces,
Ravens and vultures will pluck out our eyes.

With that the song ended, and at the last words, sung to a mournful air, the merry Bata's vigorous voice joined in with a loud shout of *"Lya-il-lyakha-il Allakh!"* finishing with shrill shriek. Then all was quiet again, except for the *tchuk, tchuk, tchuk, tchuk* and whistling of the nightingales from the garden and from behind the door the even grinding, and now and then the whiz, of iron sliding quickly along the whetstone.

Hadji Murád was so full of thought that he did not notice how he tilted his jug till the water began to pour out. He shook his head at himself and re-entered his room. After performing his morning ablutions he examined his weapons and sat down on his bed. There was nothing more for him to do. To be allowed to ride out he would have to get permission from the officer in charge, but it was not yet daylight and the officer was still asleep.

Khanefi's song reminded him of the song his mother had composed just after he was born—the song addressed to his father that Hadji Murád had mentioned to Loris-Melikov.

"Thy sword of Damascus-steel tore my white bosom;
But close on it laid I my own little boy;
In my hot-streaming blood him I laved ; and the wound
Without herbs or specifics was soon fully healed.
As I, facing death, remained fearless, so he,
My boy, my *dzhigit,* from all fear shall be free !

He remembered how his mother put him to sleep beside her under a cloak, on the roof of their *saklya,* and how he asked her to let him see the place on her side where the wound had left a scar. Hadji Murád seemed to see his mother before him—not wrinkled, grey-haired, with gaps between her teeth, as he had lately left her, but young handsome and so strong that she carried him in a basket on her back across the mountams to her father's when he was a heavy five-year-old boy. He also recalled his. grandfather, wrinkled and grey-bearded, and how the old man hammered silver with his sinewy hands, and made him say his prayers.

He thought of the fountain at the foot of the hill, whither, holding to her wide trousers, h& went with his mother to fetch water. He remembered the lean dog that used to lick his face, and he recalled with special vividness the peculiar smell of sour milk and smoke in the hed where his mother took him with her when she went to milk the cows or scald the milk.. He remembered how she shaved his head for the first time, and how surprised he was to see his round blue-gleaming head reflected in the brightly-polished brass basin that hung against the wall.

And the recollection of himself as a little child reminded him of his beloved son, Yusuf, whose head he himself had shaved for the first time; and now this Yusuf was a handsome young *dzhigit*. He pictured him as he was when last he saw him on the day he left Tselmess. Yusuf had brought him his horse and asked to be allowed to accompany him. He was ready dressed and armed, and led his own horse by the bridle, and his rosy handsome young face and the whole of his tall slender figure (he was taller than his father) breathed of daring, youth, and the joy of life. The breadth of his shoulders, though he was so young, the very side youthful hips, the long slender waist, the strength of his long arms, and the power, flexibility, and agility of all his movements had always rejoiced Hadji Murád, who admired his son.

"Thou hadst better stay. Thou wilt e alone at home now. Take care of thy mother and thy grandmother," said Hadji Murád. And he remembered the spirited and proud look and the flush of pleasure with which Yusuf had replied that as long as he lived no one should injure his mother or grandmother. All the same, Yusuf had mounted and accompanied his father as far as the stream. There he turned back, and since then Hadji Murád had not seen his wife, his mother, or his son. And it was this son whose eyes Shamil threatened to put out! Of what would be done to his wife Hadji Murád did not wish to think.

These thoughts so excited him that he could not sit still any longer. He jumped up and went limping quickly to the door, opened it, and called Eldár. The sun had not yet risen, but it was already quite light. The nightingales were still singing.

"Go and tell the officer that I want to go out riding, and saddle the horses," said he.

CHAPTER XXIV

Butler's only consolation all this time was the poetry of warfare, to which he gave himself up not only during his hours of service but also in private life. Dressed in his Circassian costume, he rode and swaggered about, and twice went into ambush with Bogdanovich, though neither time did they discover or kill anyone. This closeness to and friendship with Bogdanovich, famed for his courage, seemed pleasant and warlike to Butler. He had paid his debt, having borrowed the money of a Jew at an enormous rate of interest—that is to say, he had postponed his difficulties but had not solved them. He tried not to think of his position, and to find oblivion not only in the poetry of warfare but also in wine. He drank more and more every day, and day by day grew morally weaker. He was now no longer the chaste Joseph he had been towards marya Dmitrievna, but on the contrary began courting her grossly, meeting to his surprise with a strong and decided repulse which put him to shame.

At the end of April there arrived at the fort a detachment with which Baryatinsky intended to effect an advance right through Chechnya, which had till then been considered impassable. In that detachment were two companies of the Kabarda regiment, and according to Caucasian custom these were treated as guests by the Kurín companies. The soldiers were lodged in the barracks, and were treated not only to supper, consisting of buckwheat porridge and beef, but also to vodka. The officers shared the quarters of the Kurín officers, and as usual those in residence gave the new-comers a dinner at which the regimental singers performed and which ended up with a drinking bout. Major Petrov, very drunk and no longer red but ash pale, sat astride a chair and, drawing his sword, hacked at imaginary foes, alternately swearing and laughing, now embracing someone and now dancing to the tune of his favorite song.

Shamil, he began to riot

In the days gone by;

Try, ry, rataty,

In the years gone by!

Butler was there, too. He tried to see the poetry of warfare in this also, but in the depth of his soul he was sorry for the major. To stop him, however, was quite impossible; and Butler, feeling that the fumes were mounting to his own head, quietly left the room and went home.

The moon lit up the white houses and the stones on the road. It was so light that every pebble, every straw, every little heap of dust was visible. As he approached the house he met Marya Dmitrievna with a shawl over her head and neck. After the rebuff she had given him Butler had avoided her, feeling rather ashamed, but now in the moonlight and after the wine he had drunk he was pleased to meet her and wished again to make up to her .

"Where are you off to?"he asked.

"Why, to see after my old man,"she answered pleasantly. Her rejection of Butler's advances was quite sincere and decided, but she did not like his avoiding her as he had done lately.

"Why bother about him? He'll soon come back."

"But will he?"

"If he doesn't they'll bring him."

"Just so…That's not right, you know!…But you think I'd better not go?"

"No,don't. We'd better go home."

Marya Dmitrievna turned back and walked beside him. The moon shone so brightly that a halo seemed to move along the road round the shadows of their heads. Butler was looking at this halo and making up his mind to tell her that he liked her as much as ever, but he did not know how to begin. She waited for him to speak, and they walked on in silence almost to the house, when some horsemen appeared from round the corner. These were an officer with an escort.

"Who's that coming now?" said marya Dmitrievna, stepping aside. The moon was behind the rider so that she did not recognize him until he had almost come up to them. It was Peter Nikolaevich Kamenev, an officer who had formerly served with the major and whom Marya Dmitrievna therefore knew.

"Is it you, Peter Nikolaevich?" said she, addressing him.

"It's me," said Kamenev."ah, Butler, how d'you do?…Not asleep yet? Having a walk with Marya Dmitrievna! You'd better look out or the major will give it you…Where is he?"

"Why, there…Listen!" replied Marya Dmitrievna pointing in the direction whence came the sounds of a *tulumbas*[1] and songs. "They're on the spree."

"How's that ? Are your people having a spree on their own?"

"No;some officers have come from Hasav-Yurt, and they are being entertained."

"Ah, that's good! I shall be in time…I just want the major for a moment."

"On business?" asked Butler.

"Yes, just a little business matter."

1. Tulumbas, a sort of kettledrum.

"Good or bad?"

"It all depends…Good for us but bad for somc people," and Kamenev laughed.

By this time they had reached the major's house.

"Chikhirev," shouted Kamenev to one of his Cossacks,

"come here!"

A Don Cossack rode up from among the others. He was dressed in the ordinary Don Cossack uniform with high boots and a mantle, and carried saddle-bags behind.

"Well, take the thing out," said Kamenev, dismounting.

The Cossack also dismounted, and took a sack out of his saddle bag. Kamenev took the sack from him and put his hand in.

"Well,shall I show you a novelty? You won't be frightened, Marya Dmitrievna?"

"Why should I be frightened?" she replied.

"Here it is!" said Kamenev taking out a man's head and holding it up in the light of the moon. "Do you recognize it?"

It was a shaven head with salient brows, black shortcut beard and mustaches, one eye open and the other half-closed. The shaven skull was cleft, but not right through, and there was congealed blood in the nose. The neck was wrapped in a blood-stained towel. Notwithstanding the many wounds on the head, the blue lips still bore a kindly childlike expression.

Marya Dmitrievna looked at it, and without a word turned away and went quickly into the house.

Butler could not tear his eyes from the terrible head. It was the head of that very Hadji Murád with whom he had so recently spent his evenings in such friendly intercourse.

"How's that ? Who has killed him?"he asked.

"Wanted to give us the slip, but was caught," said Kamenev, and he gave the head back to the Cossack and went into the house with Butler.

"He died like a hero," said kamenev.

"But however did it all happen?"

"Just wait a bit. When the major comes I'll tell you all about it. That's what I am sent for. I take it round to all the forts and *aouls* and show it."

The major was sent for, and came back accompanied by two other officers as drunk as himself, and began embracing Kamenev.

"And I have brought you Hadji Murád's head," said Kamenev.

"No? … Killed?"

"Yes; wanted to escape."

"I always said he would bamboozle them!...and where is it? The head, I mean...Let's see it."

The Cossack was called, and brought in the bag with the head. It was taken out and the major looked long at it with drunken eyes.

"All the same, he was a fine fellow," said he. "Let me kiss him!"

"Yes, it's true. It was a valiant head," said one of the officers.

When all had looked at it, it was returned to the Cossack who put it in his bag, trying to let it bump against the floor as gently as possible.

"I say, Kamenev, what speech do you make when you show the head?" asked an officer.

"No!...Let me kiss him. He gave me a sword!" shouted the major.

Butler went out into the porch.

Marya Dmitrievna was sitting on the second step. She looked round at Butler and at once turned angrily away again.

"What's the matter, marya Dmitrievna?"asked he.

"You're all cut-throats!...I hate it! You're cut-throats, really," and she got up.

"It might happen to anyone," remarked Butler, not knowing what to say. "That's war."

"War? War, indeed!...Cut-throats and nothing else. A dead body should be given back to the earth, and they're grinning at it there!...Cut-throats, really," she repeated, as she descended the steps and entered the house by the back door.

Butler returned to the room and asked Kamenev to tell them in detail how the thing had occurred.

And Kamenev told them.

This is what had happened.

CHAPTER XXV

Hadji Murád was allowed to go out riding in the neighborhood of the town, but never with out a convoy of Cossacks. There was only half a troop of them altogether in Nukha, ten of whom were employed by the officers, so that if ten were sent out with Hadji Murád (according to the orders received) the same men would have had to go every other day. Therefore after ten had been sent out the first day, it was decided to send only five in future, and Hadji Murád was asked not take all his henchmen with him. But on April the 25th he rode out with all five. When he mounted, the commander, noticing that all five henchmen were going with him, told him that he was forbidden to take them all, but Hadji Murád pretended not to hear, touched his horse, and the commander did not insist.

With the Cossacks rode a non-commissioned officer, Nazarov, who had received the Cross of St. George for bravery. He was a young, healthy, brown-haired lad, as fresh as a rose. He was the eldest of a poor family belonging to the sect of Old Believers, had grown up without a father, and had maintained his old mother, three sisters, and two brothers.

"Mind, Nazarov, keep close to him!" shouted the commander.

"All right, your honour!" answered Nazarov, and rising in his stirrups and adjusting the rifle that hung at his back, he started his fine large roan gelding at a trot. Four Cossacks followed him: therapontov, tall and thin, a regular thief and plunderer (he it was he who had sold gunpowder to Gamzálo); Ignatov, a sturdy peasant who boasted of his strength, though he was no longer young and had nearly completed his service; Mishkin, a weakly lad at whom everybody laughed; and the young fair-haired Petrakov, his mother's only son, always amiable and jolly.

The morning had been misty, but it cleared up later on and the opening foliage, the young virgin grass, the sprouting corn, and the ripples of the rapid river just visible to the left of the road, all glittered in the sunshine.

Hadji Murád rode slowly along followed by the Cossacks and by his henchmen. They rode out along the road beyond the fort at a walk. They met women carrying baskets on their heads, soldiers driving carts, and creaking wagons drawn by buffaloes. When he had gone about a mile and a half Hadji Murád touched up his white Kabarda horse, which started at an amble that obliged the henchmen and Cossacks to ride at a quick trot to keep up with him.

"Ah, he's got a fine horse under him," said therapontov. "If only he were still an enemy I'd soon bring him down."

"Yes, mate. Three hundred rubles were offered for that horse in Tiflis."

"But I can get ahead of him on mine," said Nazarov.

"You get ahead? A likely thing!"

Hadji kept increasing his pace.

"Hey, *kunak*, you mustn't do that. Steady!" cried Nazarov, starting to overtake Hadji Murád.

Hadji Murád looked round, said nothing, and continued to ride at the same pace.

"Mind, they're up to something, the devils!" said Ignatov. "See how they are tearing along."

So they rode for the best part of a mile in the direction of the mountains.

"I tell you it won't do!" shouted Nazarov.

Hadji Murád did not answer, or look round, but only increased his pace to a gallop.

"Humbug! You won't get away!" shouted Nazarov, stung to the quick. He gave his big roan gelding a cut with his whip and, rising in his stirrups and bending forward, flew full speed in pursuit of Hadji Murád.

The sky was so bright, the air so clear, and life played so joyously in Nazarov's soul as, becoming one with his fine strong horse, he flew along the smooth road behind Hadji Murád, that the possibility of any thing sad or dreadful happening never occurred to him. He rejoiced that with every step he was gaining on Hadji Murád.

Hadji Murád judged by the approaching tramp of the big horse behind him that he would soon be overtaken, and seizing his pistol with his right hand, with his left he began slightly to rein in his Kabarda horse which was excited by hearing the tramp of hoofs behind it.

"You mustn't, I tell you!" shouted Nazarov, almost level with Hadji Murád and stretching out his hand to seize the latter's bridle. But before he reached it a shot was fired. "What are you doing?" he screamed catching Nazarow, at his breast. "At them, lads!" and he reeled and fell forward on his saddle bow.

But the mountaineers were beforehand in taking to their weapons, and fired their pistols at the Cossacks and hewed at them with their swords.

Nazarov hung on the neck of his horse, which careered round his comrades. the horse under Ignatov ell, crushing his leg, and two of the mountaineers, without dismounting, drew their swords and hacked at his head and arms. Petrakov was about to rush to his comrade's rescue when two shots—one in his back and the other in his side—stung him, and he fell from his horse like a sack.

Mishkin turned round and galloped off towards the fortress. Khanefi and Bata rushed after him, but he was already too far away and they could not catch him. When they saw that they could not overtake him they returned to the others.

Petrakov lay on his back, his stomach ripped open, his young face turned to the sky, and while dying he gasped for breath like a fish.

Gamzálo having finished off Ignatov with his sword, gave a cut to Nazarov too and threw him from his horse. Bata took their cartridge-pouches from the slain. Khanefi wished to take Nazarov's horse, but Hadji Murád called out to him to leave it, and dashed forward along the road. His *murids* galloped after him, driving away Nazarov's horse that tried to follow them. they were already among rice-fields more than six miles from Nukha when a shot was fired from the tower of that place to give the alarm.

* * * * *

"Oh good lord! Oh dear me! Dear me! What have they done?" cried the commander of the fort seizing his head with his hands when he heard of Hadji Murád's escape. "They've done for me! They've let him escape, the villains!" cried he, listening to Mishkin's account.

An alarm was raised everywhere and not only the Cossacks of the place were sent after the fugitives but also all the militia that could be mustered from the pro-Russian aouls. A thousand rubles reward was offered for the capture of Hadji Murád alive or dead, and two hours after he and his followers had escaped from the Cossacks more than two hundred mounted men were following the officer in charge at a gallop to find and capture the runaways.

After riding some miles along the high road Hadji Murád checked his panting horse, which, wet with sweat, had turned from white to grey.

To the right of the road could be seen the *sáklya*s and minarets of the aoul Benerdzhik, on the left lay some fields, and beyond them the river. Although the way to the mountains lay to the right, Hadji Murád turned to the left, in the opposite direction, assuming that his pursuers would be sure to go to the right, while he, abandoning the road, would cross the Alazan and come out onto the high road on the other side, where no one would expect him—ride along it to the forest, and then after recrossing the river make his way to the mountains.

Having come to this conclusion he turned to the left; but it proved impossible to reach the river. The rice-field which had to be crossed had just been flooded, as is always done in spring, and had become a bog in which the horses's legs sank above their pasterns. Hadji Murád and his henchmen turned now to the left, now to the right, hoping to find drier ground; but the field they were in had been equally flooded all over and was now saturated with water. The horses drew their feet out of the sticky mud into which they sank, with a pop like that of a cork drawn from a bottle, and stopped, panting, after every few steps. They struggled in this way so long that it began to grow dusk and they had still not reached the river. To their left lay a patch of higher ground overgrown with shrubs and Hadji Murád decided to ride in among these clumps and remain there till night to rest their worn-out horses and let them graze. The men themselves at some bread and cheese they had brought with them. At last night came on and the moon that had been shining at first, hid behind the hill and it be130 came dark. There were a great many nightingales in that neighbourhood and there were two of them in these shrubs. As long as Hadji Murád and his men were making a noise among the bushes the nightingales had been silent, but when the people became still the birds again began to call to one another and to sing.

Hadji Murád, awake to all the sounds of night, listened to them involuntarily, and their trills reminded him of the song about Hamzad which he had heard the night before when he went to get water. He might now at any moment find himself in the position in which Hamzad had been. He fancied that it would be so, and suddenly his soul became serious. He spread out his *búrka* and performed his ablutions, and scarcely had he finished before a sound was heard approaching their shelter. It was the sound of many horses' feet splashing through the bog.

The keen-sighted Bata ran out to one edge of the clump, and peering through the darkness saw black shadows, which were men on foot and on horseback. Khanefi discerned a similar crowd on the other side. It was Karganov, the military commander of the district, with his militia.

"Well, then, we shall fight like Hamzad," thought Hadji Murád.

When the alarm was given, Karganov with a troop of militiamen and Cossacks had rushed off in pursuit of Hadji Murád, but had been unable to find any trace of him. He had already lost hope, and was returning home when, towards evening, he met an old man and asked him if he had seen any horsemen about. The old man replied that he had. He had seen six horsemen floundering in the rice-field, and then had seen them enter the clump where he himself was getting wood. Karganov turned back, taking the old man with him, and seeing the hobbled horses, he made sure that Hadji Murád was there. In the night he surrounded the clump, and waited till morning to take Hadji Murád alive or dead.

Having understood that he was surrounded, and having discovered an old ditch among the shrubs, Hadji Murád decided to entrench himself in it and to resist as long as strength and ammunition lasted. He told his comrades this, and ordered them to throw up a bank in front of the ditch, and his henchmen at once se to work to cut down branches, dig up the earth with their daggers, and make an entrenchment. Hadji Murád himself worked with them. As soon as it began to grow light the commander of the militia troop rode up to a clump and shouted:

"Hey! Hadji Murád, surrender! We are many and you are few!"

In reply came the report of a rifle, a cloudlet of smoke rose from the ditch and a bullet hit the militiaman's horse, which staggered under him and began to fall. The rifles of the militiamen who stood at the outskirts of the clump of shrubs began cracking in their turn, and their bullets whistled and hummed, cutting off leaves and twigs and striking the embankment, but not the men entrenched behind it. Only Gamzálo's horse, that had strayed from the others, was hit in the head by a bullet. It did not fall, but breaking its hobbles and rushing among the bushes it ran to the other horses, pressing close to them and watering the young grass with its blood. Hadji Murád and his men fired only when any of the militiamen came forward, and rarely missed their aim. Three militiamen were wounded, and the others, far from making up their minds to rush the entrenchment, retreated farther and farther back, only firing from a distance and at random.

So it continued for more than an hour. The sun had risen to about half the height of the trees, and Hadji Murád was already thinking of leaping on his horse and trying to make his way to the river, when the shouts were heard of many men who had just arrived. These were Hadji Aga of Mekhtuli with his followers. There were about two hundred of them. Hadji Aga had once been Hadji Murád's kunak and had lived with him in the mountains, but he had afterwards gone over to the Russians. With him was Akhmet Khan, the son of Hadji Murád's old enemy.

Like Karganov, Hadji Aga began by calling to Hadji Murád to surrender, and Hadji Murád answered as before with a shot.

"Swords out, Lads!" cried Hadji Aga, drawing his own; and a hundred voices were raised by men who rushed shrieking in among the shrubs.

The militiamen ran in among the shrubs, but from behind the entrenchment came the crack of one shot after another. Some three men fell, and the attackers stopped at the outskirts of the clump and also began firing. As they fired they gradually approached the entrenchment, running across from behind one shrub to another. Some succeeded in getting across, others fell under the bullets of Hadji Murád or of his men. Hadji Murád fired without missing; Gamzálo too rarely wasted a shot, and shrieked with joy every time he saw that his bullet had hit its aim. Khan Mahoma sat at the edge of the ditch singing "*Il lyakha il Allakh!*" and fired leisurely, but often missed. Eldár's whole body trembled with impatience to rush dagger in hand at the enemy, and he fired often and at random, constantly looking round at Hadji Murád and stretching out beyond the entrenchment. The shaggy Khanefi, with his sleeves rolled up, did the duty of a servant even here. He loaded the guns which Hadji Murád and Khan Mahoma passed to him, carefully driving home with a ramrod the bullets wrapped in greasy rags, and pouring dry powder out of the powder-flask on to the pans. Bata did not remain in the ditch as the others did, but kept running to the horses, driving them away to a safer place, and shrieking incessantly, fired without using a prop for his gun. He was the first to be wounded. A bullet entered his neck and he sat down spitting blood and swearing. Then Hadji Murád was wounded, the bullet piercing his shoulder. He tore some cotton wool from the lining of his *beshmet,* plugged the wound with it, and went on firing.

"Let us fly at them with our swords!" said Eldár for the third time, and he looked out from behind the bank of earth ready to rush at the enemy; but at that instant a bullet struck him and he reeled and fell backwards on to Hadji Murád's leg. Hadji Murád glanced at him. His beautiful eyes, like those of a gazed intently and seriously at Hadji Murád. His mouth, the upper lip pouting like a child's, twitched without opening. Hadji Murád drew his leg away from under him and continued firing.

Khanefi bent over the dead Eldár and began taking the unused ammunition out of the cartridge cases of his coat.

Khan Mahoma meanwhile continued to sing, loading leisurely and firing. The enemy ran from shrub to shrub, hallooing and shrieking and drawing ever nearer and nearer.

Another bullet hit Hadji Murád in the left side. He lay down in the ditch and again pulled some cotton wool out of his *beshmet* and plugged the wound. This wound in the side was fatal and he felt that he was dying. Memories and pictures succeeded one another with extraordinary rapidity in his imagination. now he saw the powerful Abu Nutsal Khan, dagger in hand and holding up his severed cheek as he rushed at his foe; then he saw the weak, bloodless old Vorontsóv with his cunning white face, and heard his soft voice; then he saw his son Yusuf, his wife Sofiat, and then the pale, red-bearded face of his enemy Shamil with its half-closed eyes. All these images passed through his mind without evoking any feeling within him—neither pity nor anger nor any kind of desire: everything seemed so insignificant in comparison with what was beginning, or had already begun, within him.

Yet his strong body continued the thing that he had commenced. Gathering together his last strength he rose from behind the bank, fired his pistol at a man who was just running towards him, and hit him. The man fell. Then Hadji Murád got quite out of the ditch, and limping heavily went dagger in hand straight at the foe.

Some shots cracked and he reeled and fell. Several militiamen with triumphant shrieks rushed towards the fallen body. But the body that seemed to be dead suddenly moved. First the uncovered, bleeding, shaven head rose; then the body with hands holding to the trunk of a tree. He seemed so terrible, that those who were running towards him stopped short. But suddenly a shudder passed through him, he staggered away from the tree and fell on his face, stretched out at full length like a thistle that had been mown down, and he moved no more.

He did not move, but still he felt.

When Hadji Aga, who was the first to reach him, struck him on the head with a large dagger, it seemed to Hadji Murád that someone was striking him with a hammer and he could not understand who was doing it or why. That was his last consciousness of any connection with his body. He felt nothing more and his enemies kicked and hacked at what had no longer anything in common with him.

Hadji Aga placed his foot on the back of the corpse and with two blows cut off the head, and carefully— not to soil his shoes with blood—rolled it away with his foot. Crimson blood spurted from the arteries of the neck, and black blood flowed from the head, soaking the grass.

Karganov and Hadji Aga and Akhmet Khan and all the militiamen gathered together—like sportsmen round a slaughtered animal—near the bodies of Hadji Murád and his men (Khanefi, Khan Mahoma, and Gamzálo they bound), and amid the powder-smoke which hung over the bushes they triumphed in their victory.

The nightingales, that had hushed their songs while the firing lasted, now started their trills once more: first one quite close, then others in the distance.

* * * * *

It was of this death that I was reminded by the crushed thistle in the midst of the ploughed field.

Gyan Books 11298/3/11/17